PENGUIN BOOKS
SATYR OF THE SUBWAY

Anita Nair lives in Bangalore and Mundakotukurussi, Kerala. Her books have been translated into over twenty-five languages around the world. Visit her at www.anitanair.net.

Praise for *The Better Man* (1999)

'*The Better Man* is an astonishing book. It is tender, lyrical, humorous and insightful' — Abraham Verghese, author of *The Tennis Partner* and *My Own Country*

'A genial, meandering tale... Charming' — *New York Times Sunday Book Review*

'This imaginative debut will delight with its remarkable grace, unforced humour and elegantly descriptive prose' — *Library Journal*

'Nair has the magical ability to make all her readers feel, briefly, like Kaikurussi villagers in this humorous, imaginative and gracefully written novel' — *Publishers Weekly*

'Imposing debut: Nair's got a style and a future... Rich in local colour...explored in fluid prose. Anita Nair has proved her mettle by fathoming the deepest recesses of man's psyche...' — *India Today*

'A simple tale simply told. A first novel of great promise... Kaikurussi, one-tea-shop town somewhere in Kerala, comes alive with Nair's pen... Doesn't pander to prefab audiences or juries and conforms only to its own contours' — *Indian Review of Books*

Praise for *Ladies Coupé* (2001)

'A brilliant evocation of sisterhood on the move... Nair's tale is light enough to relieve the tedium of a long journey and yet filled with the incantatory power to burn up tracks, to seek a new destination. To change' — *India Today*

'Anita Nair's second novel upholds the promise of the first... Each of the women are finely drawn [as are their men], each caught in a net of relationships partly of her own making and partly one that is "made" for her... Anita Nair's low key, sometimes funny and sometimes hard-hitting book...is definitely worth a read' — Urvashi Butalia, *The Hindustan Times*

'Anita Nair is a fine writer with a great sense of character, vivid knowledge of South Indian culture and an eye for telling detail. She can move from tender compassion to sensuality to raging hatred and is a compelling teller of stories' — *The Hindu Literary Supplement*

'Her strength as a writer lies in bringing alive the everyday thoughts, desires and doubts' — *Times Literary Supplement*, London

'Nair is a powerful writer: all of these stories are intense and replete with cultural detail... Nair has created what must be one of the most important feminist novels to come out of South Asia' — *The Daily Telegraph,* UK

'These women's life stories give an insight into expectations of married Indian women, the choices they make and the choices made for them. Anita Nair's story-telling is superb and each woman could easily spawn a novel of her own... There is a strong message of hope through change and even the ending is revealed as another beginning. Enticing and uplifting' — *Punch*

Praise for *Mistress* (2005)

'Nair makes art a living experience, literally... When the performers in *Mistress* realize that they have to discard the costume to regain their humanity, it is too late. The art of Anita Nair does it for them in style' — *India Today*

'With her first two novels, *The Better Man* and *Ladies Coupé*, Anita Nair signalled the arrival of a sensitive writer who could delve deep into people's personalities and take the reader on a wonderful journey. With her latest book *Mistress*, she lives upto the promise of a masterful storyteller...' — *The Times of India*

'Set in Kerala, spanning 90 years, Nair's third novel explores the depths of relationships while, in a parallel strand, it unravels the skeins that weave together a life in art... Nair's narrative powers and mastery of minutiae remain her forte...this novel proves she is conscious of the trivialisation of art, a mistress who accepts no compromises' — *The Hindu*

'*Mistress* is a well-written novel that gifts the reader with knowledge of a magical art form. For that reason it should be read by all, from the uncompromising artist to the champions of contemporaneous India' —— *Tehelka*

'Fiction and research go hand in hand in *Mistress*, Anita Nair's latest book…an absorbing story of two plots that run parallel, almost at the same pace… Kathakali, the exacting, vibrant dance form of Kerala, may seem to appeal to a niche segment. But the author has given its colour and character an appeal that cuts across geographical boundaries' —— *The Asian Age*

'*Mistress* turns around its titillating title to make an evocative look at human relationships under the magnifying lens of art' —— *The Week*

'Like a true Kathakali spectacle performed by master veshakaars that lasts all night, Nair evokes in her readers wonder, delight and grief. She writes about man-woman relationships and complex Kathakali aesthetics with equal felicity. When you put down the novel, you feel as if you are walking back home in the pale early morning light at the end of a nightlong Kathakali performance. What fills your soul, then, is shaantam—the last of the nine bhavas' —— M. Mukundan, *The Hindu Literary Review*

satyr of the subway

URBAN TALES

Anita Nair

PENGUIN BOOKS

PENGUIN BOOKS
Published by the Penguin Group
Penguin Books India Pvt. Ltd, 11 Community Centre, Panchsheel Park, New
Delhi 110 017, India
Penguin Group (USA) Inc., 375 Hudson Street, New York, New York 10014,
USA
Penguin Group (Canada), 90 Eglinton Avenue East, Suite 700, Toronto,
Ontario, M4P 2Y3, Canada (a division of Pearson Penguin Canada Inc.)
Penguin Books Ltd, 80 Strand, London WC2R 0RL, England
Penguin Ireland, 25 St Stephen's Green, Dublin 2, Ireland (a division of Penguin
Books Ltd)
Penguin Group (Australia), 250 Camberwell Road, Camberwell, Victoria
3124, Australia (a division of Pearson Australia Group Pty Ltd)
Penguin Group (NZ), cnr Airborne and Rosedale Roads, Albany, Auckland
1310, New Zealand (a division of Pearson New Zealand Ltd)
Penguin Group (South Africa) (Pty) Ltd, 24 Sturdee Avenue, Rosebank,
Johannesburg 2196, South Africa

Penguin Books Ltd, Registered Offices: 80 Strand, London WC2R 0RL,
England

First published by Penguin Books India 2006

Copyright © Anita Nair 2006

Twelve of the stories featured in this volume were originally published in
slightly modified form in *Satyr of the Subway and Eleven Other Stories* by
Haranand Publications Pvt. Ltd, 1997.

All rights reserved
10 9 8 7 6 5 4 3 2 1

ISBN-13: 978-0-14309-965-9   ISBN-10: 0-14309-965-5

Typeset in Perpetua by Mantra Virtual Services, New Delhi
Printed at Saurabh Printers Pvt. Ltd, Noida

CONTENTS

For Dr P.K. Sunil

&

for Franklin Bell, Jayanth Kodkani & Patrick Wilson

~

satyr of the subway

There is a world that huddles beneath the feet of every New Yorker. A subterranean realm of acrid grey, steamy lime and greasy fumes. In this devil basement, dank steel caterpillars, christened with molten metal alphabets on their deadpan foreheads, prowl hither and thither. Opening hungry mouths on either side, trapping the manic lemmings who rush in, part of a mass suicide drive. See how they clutch at coats, bags and attaché cases with a foetal grip. Eyes glazed, these feral creatures hang on to the innards of the steel worm.

Minutes later, this human cud is regurgitated and spat out with the vehemence of a cereal box spewing rice krispies into a breakfast bowl. Inward-turned, shifty-eyed, conducting conversations in normal voices with themselves, they ignore the lure of contact and meander into the underground passages that will in turn lead them to the promise of sunshine. Meanwhile, here time stands still, the music is tenor sax and the poems charcoal obscenities scrawled on a wall the colour of a festering bruise.

It is here that I, part-man, part-goat, search for my inspiration, my muse, my maiden of the woods, meadows and oracle groves.

In the whorehouse called the solar system, the sun plays the role of the Madam, holding the vagrant girls together in a state of orderliness by the sheer strength of her charisma. A power the human world often contemptuously dismisses as gravitational pull.

However, every once in a while, for a few days, the sun takes a sort of vacation. Mostly she sups on broth and hides behind fleecy quilts, recouping from wearing a bright countenance almost non-stop. Just so the girls don't forget who is boss, she shows herself for a few minutes before retiring to her slumber room once again.

Every day, when the sun is steeling herself to shine on for a few hours more, I wipe the paint off my brushes, lay them gently in their pot, dry my hands, don my hat and walk into the womb of my subterranean mother.

My real one resides in a little blue crock on my mantelpiece. My mother, for whom life was a marrow bone to suck till the last morsel had whistled down her throat, died in a manner that befitted her life: she choked on a marrow bone. Momma, who was the quintessential mother with a flowing bosom, a tiered waist and an iron will, sat there gasping before me and I let her die. She was much too big for me to attempt the Heimlich manoeuvre.

When Momma was RIP in the blue crock she'd loved so much, I sat in the chintz-covered armchair that she had guarded after Poppa died, and contemplated my future. I was forty-five years old, owned a sizeable chunk of real estate in New Jersey, had an unstimulating, non-invigorating job and a bouquet garni for a name.

Momma's womb had refused to flower until an old woman she knew back home in her village in Syria, sent her a bittersweet potion. It let loose the dragons in Momma's womb and allowed a tiny tadpole entry to grow and flourish. And so, Momma

Satyr of the Subway

became a mum and I, Basil Bayleaf.

The magic potion had included the two herbs and Momma rather liked the ring of Basil Bayleaf. 'It's a name with a meaning, pet,' she would say. 'Basil means royal and the bayleaf, when not flavouring soups, was used to wreathe the heads of poets and scholars.'

Poppa was too son-struck to do anything about it, and so I was left to live like a true bouquet garni. There, and not there.

After Momma died, I quit my job and moved to Manhattan. I found myself a suite of rooms on West 54th. There was a restaurant called Russia Tea House in the same block and the Lincoln Center was close by. The streets were busy, my living space cramped, the phone never rang, and I was where I wanted to be—with Momma at touching distance and yet not so close as to go in her dulcet gutturals all day: 'Basil, my son, surely you don't want to be seen wearing a shirt like that.' 'My pet, it is time you switched to your thermal underwear. We don't want to be catching a cold, do we?'

I was free. I was free to do as I wanted. Free to paint. I could do a good likeness of people's faces. So, once in a while, I let the gods of commerce coerce me into doing a portrait of some sombre being. I painted it solemnly and without joy. I would mount it in a gilt frame and deposit my cheque at the Hanovers Manufacturers Bank. And then I would skip back to my easel, to paint my obsession over and over again.

In the sea of anatomy, each man chooses a resting place for himself. An isle that he nets into every fantasy. The spot his eye is drawn to naturally, every time a woman crosses his path, be it his mother or his neighbour's wife...

There are breasts and buttocks. Cunts and clits. Legs and lips. The curve of an elbow, the length of a toenail. The slope of a cheek, the dip of a chin. And yet, it was none of these that swelled my thermal underwear or the paisley-printed silk bikini briefs I wear these days. It was the orifice god has blessed every man and every woman with. That every Jew, every Mongol, every Eskimo, every human being is born with. The impression of equality, the dent to tell us no human being is perfect or better than another.

It has a soul of its own, this once source of sustenance. This gentle sink hole of my fantasy. The navel.

There are navels and navels. The tight-lipped mutation on otherwise perfect baby skin. The anonymous slit on the child. The new-moon curve on the nubile maiden. The dead eye on the pregnant woman's convex abdominal arc. And the mysterious deep carvern; how deep is deep, one finger or two, of the woman with pomegranate hips and undulating waist? Hers is the navel of heaven. Hers is the lure of the enchantress.

Girdleless, slip-shorn, the gentle swell of her stomach textured by skin of sheer creamy linen: an outline of this ancient deep haunts me. It is this enchanted cavern I seek.

Every afternoon for two hours, I search for her amidst waves of waists. Often, I have been deceived into thinking that my quest is over. And that the perfect navel has led me to my perfect woman.

But it isn't long before I discover that the woman, like her navel, has no depth.

For over a week now, I've been in a continual state of priapic escalation. All my nerve-ends have lives of their own. I think I have at last found her.

She sat in the seat next to me that December afternoon, her fragrance that of spices, her honey-brown skin gleaming, her fingers painted ashes of rose.

When she stood up, beneath the layers of clothing, I could sense the ripeness of her hips. I followed her into the biting

4   *Satyr of the Subway*

cold of the street. Her cloud of midnight hair led me on...

For over a week now, I have been divining pieces of her life. She is a student; a hostess at an Indian restaurant; has a fondness for roasted chestnuts, and in this city filled with illiterates whose idea of self-improvement is one hour of Oprah Winfrey every day, she likes to read.

Every afternoon I watch her saunter to the bookseller on West 82nd. There, standing amidst the books on the sidewalk, she browses, she flips pages, she ponders and walks away reluctantly. And I plan my next move.

Opportunity comes as though ordained by destiny. As she stands in the subway, jostled this way and that by the crush of people eager to get in and get out, I inch my way closer to her. When I am close enough to inhale her exotic fragrance—clove and sandalwood pounded into a paste with the oil of jasmine and rubbed into cinnamon dust—I allow her a glimpse of the book I am pretending to read.

I see the flicker of interest in her eyes, her growing enthusiasm to get a closer look at the pages of my book. (Dear Mr Updike, how can I thank you for what you've done for me?) I make it easier for her to read. Now that I've interested her enough, I change my position so that the book jacket with its message in neon lighting is clearly visible. *Marry me*, the book says.

I sense the mercury shoot up into her cheeks and lodge there with a fiery glow.

For the day, I reckon, this should suffice. She will never miss me in any crowd. Maybe she will even begin to look for me...

The next day.

The subway isn't so full. And there she is. Impoverished,

lonely and book-hungry.

I murmur, 'Hi, how're ya doin?' Her eyes widen and she mumbles something back.

I woo her like the hero in a two-dollar trashy romance. I woo her with the ardent fervour of a medieval knight. I woo her in the fever pitch of a man with an ulterior motive. She intrigues me. I would like to put her in a crystal bottle and keep her close to my heart.

I know my age doesn't bother her. Maybe she even feels safe with me.

Today is the first free day she's had after she met me. We go to the Rockefeller Centre. We watch the skaters in the rink. Their feet move on the ice with the ease of a brush on canvas. A whorl of motion so perfect that my eyes begin to smart.

It's time for us to move on. I've planned a little picnic. I lead her down into my familiar world. My little hamper is incongruous and yet, right for the setting. We ride the subway all over the island and into the boroughs, switching trains as the Walkman pipes the music of the humming birds into our ears.

Life whistles past us, eyeing us strangely, and in this zone where nothing excites attention, quirks an eyebrow curiously. But we don't care.

I pour wine into long-stemmed tulip glasses and flick drops of it at her eyes. Then I feed her lobster scallops and caviar bouchées, cheese tomatoes and Camembert discs, asparagus tips with prawns and tongue rolled around mushrooms... little tidbits to whet her appetite and make her plead for more. A sort of gastronomic foreplay as my fingers stir and tease her tongue. I watch her mouth open and feel the pull of its moist softness. And I realize I really can't take it any longer. I hold out a strawberry tartlet to her and bridle my desire.

On Friday, my lovely nymph, we shall frolic amidst the

stacked frames and oil paints, the turpentine bottle and my inherited chaise lounge.

It is quarter to six on the third Friday of the last month of the year. The light is failing, and from my window I watch shoppers scurry this way and that, busy mice ticking off names as they stow meaningless, gaily wrapped gifts into paper bags.

There is a self-ordained prophet at the street corner. Stray snatches of carol music mingle with his gloomy forecast. All ye who celebrate Christmas are sinners. Fire and brimstone await thee on Judgement Day.

I watch the tramp's hand go up and down as he clang-clangs his cup. A brisk movement that matches the frantic pace of the holiday season. Quarters are lavish and hands dip into pockets more easily.

Cars screech as they jump lights and the sky is the colour of dirty underwear. There is little of the stillness of the pastoral afternoon I had envisaged us gambolling through.

Yet, within my studio, all is quiet and calm. I turn the heating a little higher than I normally like it to be.

I had placed all my paintings with their faces to the wall. I don't want to startle her or make her nervous. There had been no 'Come, see my etchings' in my invitation to her. It had merely been an invitation to see the way I lived and perhaps borrow a book or two.

Minutes later, the bell rings. I open the door and there she stands, a little nervous, a little apprehensive, but mostly curious. I help her out of her coat and lead her to the chaise lounge.

She sits on it primly, knees crossed, hands in her lap. The way a woman does when, deep in her subconscious, she realizes that the man before her, given a chance, would rudely part her legs and take his fill.

She's wearing a ribbed sweater that rises gently over her

breasts. And black velvet trousers that outline her fecund hips with the grace of a potter moulding his clay.

I watch her as she talks. Little things that mean nothing. She is finding her feet and I let her. We have all the time in the world.

The room is getting warmer and soon she takes off her sweater. Beneath it she's wearing a coral pink blouse with short sleeves and a wide neck.

There are no hollows in her neck, just a pleasing fullness. Comely shoulders and golden hair on her upper arms.

'Would you like some coffee?' I ask.

She nods. 'Basil, I have something to tell you,' she says.

'What is it, my dear?' I ask.

'It's this man. He comes to the restaurant I work in. We've been sort of seeing each other.'

'So what's the problem?' I probe.

She licks her lips. She unclasps and clasps her hands. 'He's married and we have no place to meet. My relatives in Queens would write and tell my people in India if they knew I was involved with a married man. I was wondering if we could...'

Why is it I feel I'm sinking? Why is it feel like I want to cry?

'Let me think about it,' I murmur.

'You will, won't you, Basil?' she pleads. 'It's just that we're so much in love and yet, I don't want to be the reason for the break-up of his marriage.'

That, my girl, is wanting your cake and eating it to the last crumb. But I hold the thought back in my mind.

'I will,' I say. 'I'll need to organize my day. So give me a little time.'

Now that she has said what she came to say and said it to her satisfaction, she is eager to go. But no, not so soon, my lovely. I have a greater part to play in your life than just shooting honey-dipped, sugar-frosted arrows.

I walk into my little kitchenette and put the kettle on. I spoon coffee into mugs and add sugar. And something more.

When I take in the tray, I find her curled on the chaise lounge, her shoes on the floor. She has little-girl fluffy ankle socks on.

'Tell me more about him,' I say, bewildered by this masochistic streak in me.

'He's divine. He's tall and has dark hair and the most incredible blue-grey eyes...'

'He's an American?' I interrupt.

'Yes, of course. Indian men don't want relationships. They just want to fuck.'

I flinch at her choice of word. 'So, have you fucked?' I ask rudely.

She stares at me for a moment, trying to gauge my sudden harshness, the swing of mood. She looks at the carpet and mumbles, 'Yes.' And then adds cruelly, 'But not as much as we would like to.'

For minutes we don't speak. Then she comes close to me and puts her arms around me. 'Do you feel used? You shouldn't. I thought you were my friend.'

I search her eyes. Her pupils are dilated and soon she will be under my spell.

I hold her close. How well my body contours hers. I stroke her cheek and murmur, 'I don't feel used. I feel abandoned. I feel lonely. You were to be mine.'

Her body grows more languorous. I push her back gently, onto the padded clutch of the chaise lounge.

I sit beside her and with my fingers trace every feature of hers.

'My dearest, I have looked for you so hard. It's strange, but I even dreamt of your eyes...they were the limpid brown pools I sank into and then surfaced from in my oracle grove. Again and again.

'It is this mouth, these lips and tongue that have tantalized me, teased me, it seems, for ages and ages. Every time I look at them, I want to pour myself into your mouth, let your tongue curl around me and savour me.

'Your throat, this delicate throat that holds your head like an arum lily, inviting me to seek your mouth…'

When I come to her blouse, I pause. Gently I unbutton it. Too small to be harnessed and shackled by the lacy confines of a bra, her breasts like twin wantons stare at me brazenly, their smooth perfection marred by three wiry black curling hairs. Two on the left and one on the right.

I allow my palms to cup her breasts and then I tug at their dusky peaks with my teeth. But those little bumps of flesh don't hold me for too long.

With the deftness of a fishmonger prising open an oyster, I snap open the buttons of her trousers. There, nestling in the lower abdomen, is the perfect pearl. Her navel.

The ten-petalled lotus flower with a deep, dark heart. The secret cave no man can pass by without wanting to enter. The tunnel lined with golden-brown topaz, leading to the pool of serenity.

I ease her trousers off, and her panties. Fruit of the Loom. Scented with the fragrance of a woman.

I part her legs. Her pubic hair is a perfect triangle. And its apex is the key to her loveliness.

Wind-like, my fingers furrow the pubic pasture. Their crinkly static shoots to my brain.

I lower my head and taste the wetness of her soul. Salty, with an aftertaste of heaven. Food fit for the gods.

I steal from the gods the wondrous juice, this secretion of immortality. My tongue snaking deeper and deeper, greedy for more, as far as I can reach, within and beyond her as she lies dead to the world and me. But I am not to be fooled. I know she is pretending. This naiveté, this innocence, is merely a disguise, to conceal who she really is. In her, I see each one of them. All the goddesses, all the women I have known. All the honey-tongued, sweet-faced cruel bitches...

My darling, you remind me so of Ishtar whom the earth mourned by drying all its springs, but nothing will change the fact that you were a whore. The whore of Babylonia...That's what you are. Whore, whore, whore...

Do you think I don't realize how cruel you can be, Inanna, my Sumerian goddess, my resurrected light? When Dumuzi, your shepherd lover, failed to mourn your death, you banished him to the land of no return. Just as you'll sweep me out of your life when you've got what you set out to find.

You will trample all over me. Make me eat dust, won't you? That is the kind of woman you are. Eager to control, rule and then ruin... Astarte, brutal queen, with the horns of a bull, and the arrogance that comes from being the mistress of heaven, horses and chariots... Mistress of the moment because you take what you want.

How could you have chosen that man over me ? A boy— what does he know of how to love a woman? But you are also Cybele. Mother. Mummy. Mama. How you love boys with soft faces! Tell me, how do I please you, appease you... With stinging whips, by self-stimulation and splattered blood?

Look at you lying there, floating as though amidst a sea of foam, you of the beautiful buttocks... Is anything at all sacred to you? You lust after men; husbands, sons, they give themselves to you. And yet, how can I blame them? So potent is your love, your sex... my beloved Aphrodite.

It saddens me that nothing I do will ever be what you want. For all you care about is the many forms in which you can spell your power. You seek to control the world with the sacred spring that shall never dry. For you know that your power will reign, as long as tongue, finger, phallus or thought exist.

Love juices trickling down my chin, I mount her limp body and fuck her. I draw my penis out in time to pour my oblation into that ultimate orifice, her navel.

Spent, tired, I raise myself gently off her. Drawing Momma's chair close to the lounge, I sit on it and wait for her to wake up.

Outside, the shadows are long and full, the street corners dark and brooding.

Within, the air is heavy with the aroma of sex. I rise and go to my easel. I squeeze a tube of paint onto my knife. I try to paint her ravished, power-ebbed form. But I am a man who has eaten too much, a bee that has drunk too much honey, a satyr who has caught his nymph and plundered her maidenhood. I am satiated and no longer interested. Even her navel has a wilted look…

I am not going to put her clothes back on her. I want her to know that I have extracted payment.

My deceitful darling, when you wake up, you will have a choice. To pretend nothing has happened and use my home as your love nest. Or walk away from this room and switch your subway timings. Make no mistake, I shall not change my route. I shall continue to seek my muse in the subterranean world.

Meanwhile, I shall stretch my legs, close my eyes and dream of my nymph of the woods, meadows and oracle groves.

to touch a rainbow

Once in a while the clouds part, and there comes a moon with the texture of Carrara. This marble orb has powers known to wizards and witches. The power to enchant and bewitch. To transform mortals into heavenly beings and their everyday acts to sensuous excesses. Under its influence, they say, ponds have been known to become frothing seas, and when men and women ride the sea lion in these violent seas, a giant tidal wave rolls from one to the other and throws them apart to two ends of their world. Leaving them exhausted, sweat-stained and satiated.

Of one such moon, one June night, a single moonbeam stole away. Stealthily, hardly daring to breathe, the moonbeam slid through the dense foliage of the jamun tree, and insinuated itself through the cream curtains before it fell as a single shaft of light upon the floor. The whispering voices rose above the chrome-yellow and peanut-brown stripes on white of the Bombay Dyeing sheet.

Years of marriage had splotched its newness. Mosquitoes slapped against a thigh had left bloodstains. Love juices had dribbled; semen, saliva, the bodily fluids they had wed their bodies with. Stains that no detergent could wash away.

How they wasted sperm, these new Indian women. In ancient tantric sex, if sperm didn't make babies, women rubbed it on their faces. Better than moisturizers smelling of lemon grass. Better than Oil of Olay to prevent wrinkles from ridging a smooth face.

Somewhere, a cricket rubbed together its wings. Krik-krik-krik. The room was heavy with the smoke from a mosquito coil. Spiral clouds from a gleaming eye.

In this dappled room a man and a woman made love. He was sucking her breast. Male foreplay at its best. Assuage the Opedipal longings first. So go on, roll your tongue around her nipple.

'Turn around,' he whispered.

'Ummm...'

There was a long moan and a shudder. He held her as the waves of that indescribable feeling rose and fell within him. Her plump legs around him squeezed out the last vestige of that moment.

The stealthy whispers ceased. Another stain was added to the galaxy. The voices were restored to their normal pitch. The moonlight ceased to be from a fairy tale.

'It's never been like it was tonight. You make me feel immortal. You make me feel as though there is still a life waiting to be lived. You give me the courage to decide what I should do now.' He spoke softly.

'It's time we put ourselves first. It's time we did what we want to do.' She reached for his hand, reaffirming the faith the moonbeam had blessed them with.

In another room, where a benign moon cast a fat beam of light, another couple lay in bed. Entwined. A chiaroscuro of limbs and bedclothes.

She nuzzled his chin. She liked its scratchy feel. Black beard. Blue beard. Beards were nice. Bearded men nicer.

Sleep. Women sleep better after an orgasm.

'Do you think my mother's ever had an orgasm?'

He groaned. 'Why bring your mother into our bed?'

She smiled and closed her eyes. Maybe that was it. She orgasmed; her mother didn't.

He took a long time to sleep. His nose was clogged. Sex didn't clear his nose. The laws of nature always worked in reverse for him. He eased his arm from beneath her and reached for the nasal drops. Four drops. Two in each nostril did the trick. He drank some water and slid beneath the sheet towards her.

If someone were to ask him if he was content, he would tell them no. If you are happy, he told himself in the loo every morning, it isn't healthy. It means stagnation. 'Begone, you cesspool dweller!' he would cry and the mirror would cloud with steam as the shower sprayed hot water.

He had made it his choice to be unhappy. Not malcontent— that was Edgar in *King Lear*. He liked to soak his feet in a little pool of sadness. Always. It made him more creative, he said. To be racked by depression. To burst into silent sobs and wet the pillow on Sunday afternoons.

It was all part of the image. Cultivate a few eccentricities so that when you've made it big, it'll seem like a sure sign of genius. 'All creative minds are crazy,' he said, his head held pertly, his fingers combing his hair with studious carelessness.

They didn't like to think of themselves as just another couple. They were different. Saving up for a cubbyhole flat, a home theatre and kids was what everybody else did. Not the two of them. They had no peers, no materialistic ambitions.

In the morning they sat brushing denim thighs and sweaty arms.

The bus sped through the city roads, meandering sometimes into well-maintained avenues where lawns were kept emerald-green even in summer, and the houses sat stolidly. Past shopping-malls and housing complexes, until they were out of the city limits.

The village markets teemed with life. Flowers, fruit, fish and vegetables. Swathes of colour, wholesome and fresh. Down the bridge, across empty stretches of land and pools of brown water. In the distance, the satellite town was visible, so close to the city and yet so far away. Between them lay the fear of discovery.

They walked the few yards from the bus stop to her parents' home. They lived in a little bungalow surrounded by a little garden. In the front, there were a few jasmine bushes, an old jamun tree and two lemon trees. A male and a female tree, her mother said. The female flowered and burst into fruit while the male brooded and grew more dense over the years.

The hibiscus hedge was in bloom. The street had five other houses like theirs. Everybody who lived there knew everything about everybody else. It was like a family segmented into six.

He rang the bell. It had a musical chime. London Bridge is falling down. The next caller would hear *Que sera sera*. Mother opened the door. Mother's skin had a sheen to it even though her hair was graying and needed to be touched occasionally by the beautician's expert hands. When she spoke, her eyes danced with merriment. She laughed easily and loudly. And yet, there was a strain of suppressed resentment, as if life hadn't been very fair to her.

She never could figure out why. Was it her father? Stern and stony, with stubby fingers. When he was a little drunk, his inhibitions were locked in the closet and he let his humour show. When she was away from them, in the uncertain light of the dusk or dawn, they always seemed nicer than they actually were, she thought. It didn't seem too bad then, their floundering in the kitchen sink of monotony, their wanting the approval of the world and God for themselves and their children.

She stood preening before the mirror. A small woman, with peaches for breasts, Botticelli thighs and fourteen freckles on her nose. The hairs on her arms were golden strands. She often considered removing them but it seemed too much like what her mother in her suburban life did. Pluck her eyebrows, wax her limbs, pamper her feet… Every day in every way, she sought to distance herself from her mother. She hated it if someone said, 'You resemble your mother'.

'It's just the bones and the genes, the rest of it is me,' she would protest.

She turned from the mirror. 'Mom, how do I look?'

'Like you've always done,' her mother replied lackadaisically, as she cleared the table.

'You would look more presentable if you wore better clothes,' her father broke in.

'What do you mean by better clothes?' she asked coldly.

'Not these,' he gestured, taking in her crumpled jeans and patchy T-shirt with distaste.

She watched his gaze shift to her husband. He seemed to say, not this either. But then, sons-in-law, like Caesar's wife, are above reproach.

She turned away in disgust when he added, 'What will our neighbours think?'

The bathroom was her retreat, her solace in times of seething anger.

There was something soothing about feeding her skin oils, caressing it with fragrant lather, massaging it with the abrasive pores of the loofah, perfuming and talking to herself. Love thy self before thou taketh on the world.

Sunday was one day she didn't need to think of her job in a multimedia design firm, with a bunch of cretins sucking on each other's toes and burping on bellyfuls of air.

The bathroom was a refuge. What could she talk to her parents about? Her job? CD-ROMs didn't fit within their scheme of things. Besides, they didn't understand what it was all about.

She could talk to them of the house they were planning to buy, two streets away from this one. Or her brother, the electronics engineer with a company of his own, which manufactured designer switches. But the pride in their voice as they talked of him grated on her nerves.

A smoke. A nice long smoke, she thought disjointedly.

But she couldn't really escape her parents. Like he did, pretending to sleep or read. He was a coward. She framed the questions in her mind, as she came tingling from the tip of her shaggy head to her long blunt toes.

Then lunch called a halt and there was reprieve for another few hours.

Sundays were so boring. There was nothing to do except sleep. Come to think of it, this was what they toiled all week for. The luxury of rice for lunch and the nap after.

Sunday afternoons. Lying on the iron bed that creaked if you wriggled your toes. The evening then seemed so far, and tomorrow, a light-year away.

The bed sagged in the middle and the gentle sloping hollow encouraged their bodies to seek each other. And then, there was the excitement of the open windows. Anybody could look in and see them, entwined naked.

Not for them the hasty jabs, the skirt bunched at the waist, the blouse half-open. That's rape, they said; we make love.

And making love was a ritual. Baby-talk. Clothes off. Foreplay. The slow strokes. Up down. Up down. A tightening of grip. A glassiness of eye. The pounding of blood. The waves of feeling as they swamped each nerve end. The orgasm was a second in heaven.

Sunday afternoons were cloudy great masses of grey. Fat lumps of weekend bliss. The relief breathed out by millions hung low in the sky. She lay on the bed, staring out. He slept. Soon, so did she. Dribbling into the pillow, dreaming technicolour nightmares, the result of a huge mutton-curry-and-rice lunch.

At half past four, Mother thumped on the door. She never knocked.

The lunch hung heavy in their stomachs. She had fantastic intestines. They broke down and absorbed all that she ate. Her body was methodical. Her ears accumulated little wax, her blood was red enough, even her ovaries behaved...

Not his. His scalp rained dandruff on his pimpled shoulders. His nose congested, his ears blocked and his digestion was terrible. He ran in and out of lavatories, johns, loos, toilets, or whatever name was given to a room that held a commode and cistern. A million amoebae had taken permanent residence within him. Now he pleaded for an anti-flatulence tablet.

Tea came. Hot, strong and sweet. Sip. Sip. Sip. She liked her mother's tea. There was something comforting about Brooke Bond Red Label brewed in her mother's kitchen.

She didn't make tea; he did. With the finest Darjeeling tea leaves. It's like us, she thought, very inadequate.

Sunday evenings were depressing: the thought of work, of having to cook and clean. Of having to be a wife.

Mother liked being a wife. It suited her.

They sat there in the living room, waiting for her. They loved her very much even if she didn't make them happy or proud. They waited for the weekend, for her to come home. Then it seemed like nothing had changed.

She went to sit on the new sofa. 'Don't put your feet up,' her mother remonstrated.

Mother hated dirt, untidiness. Once, long ago, her brother, sulking at having to clean his room, had said it was Freudian. This compelling urge to conquer dirt, to control some aspect of life. She had laughed. Now she wasn't so sure.

Mother sat in her armchair, her face touched with an eerie underwater tinge in the light shed by the TV screen. Father spread himself upon a matching armchair. They sat close to each other, like they had done for thirty-five years now. She didn't understand it.

'Why do you huddle together like this?' she remarked.

Mother had a strange smile on her face.

'We've been together a long time. And now that we don't have many years left together, we like to be within touching distance. We only have each other, you see. We like that reassurance.'

She felt a lump in her throat. Oh Mummy, Mummy, she wanted to cry and hide her head in her mother's lap. But she was not given to displays of affection. So she hastily changed the subject to drown her voluble emotions.

'Have you finalized the house deal?'

They looked at each other, her mother and father.

Then her mother said gently, 'We've decided not to buy that house.'

'Oh good,' she broke in cheerfully. 'Frankly, it didn't make any sense for you to move two streets away just for an extra room.'

'I didn't say we're staying on here…'

'Then?'

Her father spoke, hesitantly, searching for every word before he exposed his dream, their dream, to this callous child of theirs.

'We are going away from here. We're going back to my village. We'll build a house there. A house where I can sit and watch the rain fall. There will be no windows looking into my home, no sounds of children screaming, like here. It will be just the two of us, surrounded by trees and flowers.'

She shook her head in disbelief. 'That is a dream, an impossible dream. What's wrong with you? You'll be bored. You'll hate it. Besides, where will I go during the weekends if you go away?'

'Look,' her mother spoke angrily, 'we aren't asking you for permission. We know exactly what this move means. But it is our dream. And our choice. All our lives we've watched others, our peers, our friends, even you children plunder life, making of it what you wanted. And we were content to flow with the stream because we didn't want to upset anyone. Especially not you.

'This is our last opportunity, and we're not going to our death wondering if we made a mistake living the way we did. For once, we're not going to play safe. The house has to be built.'

'The house is going to take a while to build, so you can come here as long as we are here. And after that, you can come there, to the new house, when you have more time to spare. Don't worry, we'll be all right,' her father added kindly.

In the bus, her eyes misted once more. She looked at him sitting beside her. His face was inscrutable. The Buddha. Deadpan. Indifferent.

What will I do when they're gone, she thought over and over again.

Sunday nights were horrible. Depressing. Even the moon had gone away on holiday instead of riding with her as it did usually, grinning from ear to ear, perched on a fluffy cloud. She wished now that she had put her arms around her parents. Showed them that she wished them success with their dream. Told them she loved them.

Life was so hard. And it was so difficult not knowing what was right, what was wrong. The wind blew in her face. The buses were like enraged demons, breaking columns of the night, screeching as they sped.

She closed her eyes to thrust away the thoughts that niggled and worried with the insistence of a cavity-ridden molar.

The young still have the comfort of sleep, her parents would have said.

the witch wife's tale

The witch stood at the intersection of 145th and Amsterdam Avenue and took a deep breath. The chill of the kerb perforated the ancient leather of her shoes, invaded her woollen socks and seeped into her bones. The hood of the tattered cloak fell over her eyes, an unruly fringe of tartan that resisted all attempts at discipline. She pushed it back in irritation and looked around her. Cold fingers parted the cloak and reached for her. And as she felt the ice slither into her, she realized with a little pang that her time was up.

She'd had a premonition the previous day. Something had told her it was time she set out in search. So she had slipped into her old cloak, patted the cat and left the door ajar behind her. Somewhere in this city she would find someone she could bequeath her lifetime's work to. Somewhere, she would find a soul deserving of such happiness, such power.

She had peered into the shacks that lined the foot of the Manhattan bridge. She had watched the entrance of Macy's. She had waited on a bench in Central Park, impervious to the cold and the stares. She had stood on a flight of stairs leading to a subway station. She had paced outside the Show World Center, grimacing in disgust every time a tart brushed her sleeve. She had wandered through the Port Authority Bus Terminal, searching every face for a sign. She had peeped into steakhouses, pretended to shop at supermarkets. She had been everywhere they would let her in. And now Harlem spread around her. 'Don't Walk,' the traffic light advised.

'What do you expect me to do? Fly on a broomstick?' she asked the traffic light.

On either side, the brownstones closed in on her; a tunnel of grim cliff-sides that ate into the light and caused giant swooping shadows. Acrid smoke rose from a vent swirling at her feet. The grey sidewalk stretched, beckoning in the manner of treacherous moor paths. She heard loud breathing, the thump of heavy feet behind her, and steeled herself for what was to come. Maybe if I get across it won't catch up with me, she told herself.

Recklessly, she stepped into the river of cars that roared past her. But a hand pulled her back. 'Steady!' it cried. A shoulder supported her. A kind voice thrust her towards a stray wooden crate.

The witch felt her heart sing. She reached into the dank womb of her cloak and drew out a little skin purse. She groped for the hand and thrust the bag into it. There was no time to be lost. The Great Shredder had caught up with her, and with malicious pleasure was squeezing her life away. With one last exertion of will, she dragged her voice from the Great Shredder's grip and cried, 'In this is the power to the universe.'

'What?' the voice asked.

'Take it. Here, take it,' the witch urged. 'Feed it to anyone, the President, the Pope or the plumber, and he'll be your slave forever. Make sure that you are the first person whose eyes he looks into, after you have fed it to him. And don't ever say "I love you" to him...'

The witch felt the grip tighten on her heart and could speak no more. Would the voice use the power to change her life or would it settle for quiet content? The witch keeled over and fell. And as the Great Shredder sucked her life away as if it was the last drop of a cream soda, she realized she didn't care.

Somewhere, a car door slammed with the finality of clods of freshly-dug earth falling on a coffin, as a flake of snow licked at her upturned face.

Saro went into Manny's Chicken Place and asked for a double scoop of Cherry Vanilla. Holding the cone, she walked back thoughtfully to the brownstone that housed their apartment. In the twelve weeks she had been here, each day was an ice-cream cone she licked at surreptitiously. And before she knew it, the day was over, with nothing to show for it except a feeling of guilt that lodged somewhere in her gut. She did nothing. She knew nobody. She just drifted from one morning to the other. From one ice-cream flavour to the other.

When she reached home, she crumpled the tissue, thrust it into the bin, washed her sticky fingers and switched on the TV. Oprah came on with one of her makeover programmes. She watched an obese glum woman from Ohio transform into a pleasantly plump and articulate person in a matter of minutes. But this evening, even Oprah's brand of sorcery couldn't hold her attention. At the next commercial break, Saro gave in to her curiosity.

She pulled out the skin purse from the bomber-jacket and tugged at its drawstrings. She didn't know what she expected to find: gems covered with a fine patina of dust or a cameo brooch or a few sticks of gum. She felt disappointment radiate through her at the sight of the three black pellets that lay in her palm. It seemed typical of what her life had turned into in these past few days. She nibbled at one; it tasted sour. A little like the tamarind balls her mother made at home, pounding tamarind and rock salt in the mortar before drying the mixture in the sun. She shoved the pellets back into the bag and thrust it into the purse. 'Maybe this is going to change my life.' She realized she was talking aloud again and bit back her words.

When she had first come to this city, she had been unable to stop staring every time she found someone talking aloud to themselves, in the post office, the supermarket or the subway. She had thought there could be no one more lonely than a New Yorker. These days she no longer felt troubled when she saw the intensity of such monologues. Instead, increasingly, she understood how much it helped to talk even if it was just to one's own self.

Saro tried to concentrate on the weaving images on the TV. Then she felt a queer languid feeling rise from her stomach. A tingling that pervaded her, making her feel warm, content and happy. When she heard Sushil's key turn in the lock, she sat up. For a fleeting second, their eyes met. She felt a wave of love suffuse her. She opened her arms to him, gurgling, 'You're home early.'

He looked at her in surprise. 'I thought we could go out for a drink and some pizza afterwards,' he said a little warily. Most evenings when he came home, she sat stone-faced staring at the TV. Or she would be spoiling for an argument, if she was talking.

'No, let's stay in. I'll cook. What do you fancy?'

He looked at her disbelievingly. 'Whatever you want. Something easy.'

She began pulling out stuff from the refrigerator for an elaborate meal. 'What about pulao, chicken curry, raita and pappadum?' she chirped.

'Lovely,' he called back from the bathroom.

She hummed as she chopped, sautéed and cooked.

Sushil put on some music. The voice of Nusrat Fateh Ali Khan mixed with the aromas floating in from the kitchen to conjure a memory of home. Anxious to dispel the mood before it turned cloyingly poignant, Sushil opened a bottle of rosé. When he went in to give Saro her glass, she took it from him, murmuring absently, 'Why don't you go put your feet up?'

He stared at her in surprise. 'Are you sure there is nothing I can do to help?'

Normally, she insisted that he do his share of housework, no matter how exhausting his day had been.

Later, when she had washed up and tidied the kitchen, she showered and sprayed perfume into the hollow at her throat, on the underside of her wrists and behind her knees. She stepped into the black nylon nightdress that had been his gift to her, and which she never wore because it made her skin itch. So that he may see her and desire her, she left the bedside lamp on and draped herself on the bed. When it was time for him to come to bed, she watched him as he took off his spectacles, laid them on the bedside table and crept in to lie beside her. He reached for her hand and with his other hand he turned the lamp off, plunging the room into darkness. Then he made quiet husbandly love to her. When he came with a muted grunt, he held her in his arms for a minute and whispered in her ear, 'I love you.' Then he turned on his side and fell asleep immediately.

Saro lay on her back and stared at the ceiling. The sense of doom is a curious thing. Sometimes it's a physical sensation, sometimes a feeling. When you are free from it, you feel so light that you rise like a hot air balloon, soar in the clouds, converse with the moon, tickle the stars and make rude gestures to satellites that pass your way.

Saro felt that familiar sense of doom descending upon her. Nothing was going to change. He would continue to treat her like a slave, a whore, a… what was the word… chattel. And the worst thing was, he thought he was doing the right thing. After all, he mumbled the mandatory *I love you* after every fuck.

The time on the clock radio showed 1:39, and in its light she saw the weight that held her pinned down. A limp forearm with a fuzz of fine black hair had snaked out of the bedclothes, arching itself over her middle to crucify her to the bed. She sniffed the familiar combination of cologne and body odours, and the muskiness of sex, and felt repelled. A sob pawed at her throat. She looked at the arm in anger. Then she lifted it with her thumb and forefinger and dropped it back on the chest of its owner.

She tore the nightdress off, pulled on a T-shirt and went to sit in the living room. Outside, a police car wailed. She pressed her nose to the window and tried to still her churning emotions. And as if from memory, she remembered a wrinkled old hand clawing at her fingers, a rasping voice that had mumbled, Don't ever say 'I love you'.

In the coffee bar, a Nordic god sat beside her, stirring sugar in his espresso. She stared at him from the corner of an eye. Blonde hair that glistened on the black of his leather jacket, knee-high boots with silver caps, and a shoulder that stretched into eternity. She'd been overcome with a strange longing when he'd walked past her. Such perfection, such maleness had never come her way before.

That night, when Sushil began rubbing her back, his usual signal to tell her he desired her, she ignored him. When he persisted, she pretended to be asleep. Later, in the middle of the night, he made love to her while she fantasized that it was a man with blonde locks and hard muscles who was making her toes curl in delight. In the morning, when she woke up to Sushil's gentle snores, she felt cheated. It was a feeling that persisted all morning.

When she walked with him to the subway and a tramp waved his pan in their faces saying, 'Hey Doc, got a dime for me?' Sushil retorted, 'Not today, Charlie.'

'Why does he call you Doc?' she asked.

'I guess I look like one,' he replied absently.

She looked at him, trying to fathom the meaning of what he

had just said. And it seemed like she was seeing him for the first time as he really was: not much taller than her, with short hair and beard closely trimmed; conservative clothes and closed-in walk. It was as if he wanted to merge with the crowds, and there came to her mind an image of a golden god who walked tall, each stride saying, watch me.

She went back to the coffee bar in the afternoon, hoping he would be there. A sense of urgency drummed through her as she watched him weave his way through the crowded bar, towards the counter. When he turned to speak to the waitress, she dropped the black pellet into his cup. It was so easy. She watched the cup, wondering if it would froth and foam. But it continued to steam gently. A pool of black mud, beneath which celestial fires burned.

She kept her eyes away resolutely while he drank his coffee. When his cup was empty, she commandeered his gaze to meet hers. And in his eyes she saw recognition. Hello soulmate, she gleamed. 'Hi,' he said. 'Are you from around here?'

'What do you think?' she retorted.

He grinned. 'You tell me.'

Of what should Cordelia speak?

Of love that had wandered away. Of life that was being frittered away like popcorn crumbs. Of desire that shot through her with the ardency of a D-train every time he looked her way. An hour and many coffees later, she saw his hand creep over the counter, seeking hers. The pellet seemed to have done its work. She let her hand sink into the well of his palm, and when she felt the pressure of his fingers on hers, she knew for sure that if he were to ask her to follow him to the end of the world, she would. He ran his thumb over the ball of her palm and she turned to look into his eyes, making him a promise. Oh, my love, now that I have you in my power, I'm never going to let you go.

They walked hand in hand through the streets and silently

took a train to Washington Heights. They rode the elevator to his apartment and only when they were inside did he speak. 'All afternoon I've been wanting to do this.' Then he took her in his arms and began worshipping her with his mouth.

She lay on her side, nestling her face in his shoulder, and he said, 'I have to tell you something.'

'You are bi-sexual?' she asked flippantly.

'No. I'm married,' he stated baldly.

'So am I.'

'I know. How am I going to live without you?'

'Why should you?' she asked petulantly. 'Anyway, where is your wife?'

'I don't live here. This is my friend's apartment. I have to go back. To Maryland.'

'When?' she asked.

'Soon. Tomorrow. I have a child. A boy. He is expecting me for Christmas.'

'So what about us?' she whispered. Didn't the magic of the pellet go beyond a fuck, even a glorious one such as this?

'Give me time until after Christmas, will you? Please, honey. I'll figure it out. You could come for a visit and we could work something out then.'

He pulled her against him and when they made love this time, there was a frenzy to it that overwhelmed the two of them. As if by merging their bodies, they'd locked together their individual destinies.

He called for a cab and rode with her to the brownstone. When the cab pulled in at the kerb, he held her to him and murmured, 'I'll call you. Don't forget me, will you? You know how much I…'

'Ssh, ssh…' She put a finger on his lips. 'I know. I'll be waiting for your call.'

It was only when she walked into the apartment that she remembered Sushil.

In fairy tales, enchantresses rarely have to wait. After they have cast their spell, they don't sit by the telephone staring at it, willing it to ring. They don't have to subject themselves to the indignity of being made love to while their minds go on a honeymoon. They seldom have to go through the motions of daily routine, or endure harsh self-examination, or moments of intense torture as they wonder if a spell has an expiry date.

Saro was no enchantress. But the pellets had made her feel like one. She'd thought she'd found him and had him. But it was two weeks since that night, and she was no longer sure.

Three days into the New Year, the telephone rang, smashing the silence of the evening with its persistent call. Saro felt her heart thud in nervous anticipation.

'Hello,' she spoke into the telephone hesitantly.

'Hi.' It was him. 'It's me, Neil. How're you doing?'

'Fine. Why didn't you call?' she demanded.

'I wanted to, honey. I couldn't. I had to sort out a few things first. Do you love me still?' His voice drummed into her.

'You know I do,' she whispered, in spite of being alone in the apartment. Sushil smiled at her from a photograph.

'Say it, honey.'

'I can't,' she said helplessly.

'Who's to hear you? The geraniums or the paintings in your fancy apartment?'

'I can't. I'm not alone,' she lied. 'When do I see you?' she asked, trying not to sound desperate.

'Why don't you come down in a couple of days' time? We'll take it from there...'

'I think I will. Can I call you back, telling you what time to expect me?'

'Do that,' he said. 'I'll be waiting to hear from you.'

She put down the phone and hugged her joy to herself. Suddenly, nothing mattered except being in his arms.

When you draw a circle of magic, things have a way of falling into place naturally. Sushil was in Richmond, attending an AMWAY meet. It was so easy. All she had to do was draw some money, pack a bag and leave a message on the answering machine. Just as long as she called Sushil every day, at the same time, he wouldn't even know that she'd left New York.

Before she closed the apartment door behind her, she picked up a photograph taken on their honeymoon and looked at it for a while. There had been a time when she had thought she was in love with him. Six months of being married to him, and she had realized to her horror that she didn't even like him.

Someday soon she would have to make up her mind about what she was going to do about Sushil and their marriage. But right now, it was time for the magical reunion. And so, early on a January morning, she caught the shuttle to DC and sat in her seat, nose pressed to the glass, telling herself that she was never coming back. All she had to do was remember the clause that went with the spell.

Dare one dream of a happily ever after? The answer is yes, if you in your life have ever chanced upon a fairy godmother. Saro had, and thus in her enchanted life, husbands became pumpkins and the witching-hour had no end.

Neil met her at the station, looking more like a rock-star than ever. He picked her up in his arms and drained her lips of all the insecurities that had haunted her since he'd kissed her last.

In the old, beat-up Cadillac outside sat a giant with a sheet of jet hair crowned with a Stetson, and an oriental cast to his eyes. In the driver's seat was a tiny man, his golden locks hanging to his waist. 'This is Wolf. This is Ben,' Neil introduced them.

'Where are we going?' she asked, trying to assimilate all

the sensations coursing through her into one coherent thought.

'Home,' Neil said, holding her hand.

'And where is that?' she asked curiously.

'You'll see, honey. Don't be impatient,' he murmured, nibbling her ear.

A police car cruised past and their car swerved down an alley. 'I hate cops,' Neil said, grimness clouding his eyes.

'Do you? I love them. Sometimes I think I would love to be one,' she joked.

'Did you hear that?' Neil spoke aloud to no one in particular.

'I'm sure she is joking,' Wolf murmured. 'He hasn't stopped talking about you since he came back. What have you done to him?' Wolf winked at her.

'I cast a spell on him,' Saro said truthfully. 'Didn't he tell you I am an enchantress?'

'Oh sure, what else do you do? Charm snakes? Sleep on a bed of nails? Turn men into frogs?' Wolf laughed.

'Didn't he tell you that I am a princess and used to go to school on elephant back?'

Neil chuckled and smiled at her besottedly. 'She's cute, isn't she?'

'Any time you don't want her, I'll take her on.' Wolf grinned at her, smacking his lips lasciviously.

The house was one in a row that lined the suburban street. Trees flanked the tarmac, bare black branches laden with snow. Wispy feathery branches with highlights of silver glinted in the light—Christmas tinsel no one except a diligent sun would remove. Saro stepped out of the car and thought she had never seen anything more beautiful than Neil's home.

Inside, there was no shimmery snow to hide the shabbiness. She stood in the doorway hesitantly. She surveyed the room with its faded couches, a blazing fire and a little boy in a play-suit, seeking an ally, some familiar object in this alien terrain. Then a Wolfhound puppy bounded towards her and licked her face in boisterous welcome.

'Down, Boy, down,' Neil ordered, while Wolf looked on in exasperation.

'This dog's never going to keep anyone out,' he sneered.

Neil turned around angrily. 'Whose fault is that? You're the one spoiling him.'

'Hey, hey...' Saro broke in.

'It's okay, hon,' Neil murmured. 'Come here and give me a proper hug.'

It was as if he could read her mind and saw the doubts that buzzed in there. As she laid her cheek against his chest, she felt a pair of eyes stare at her. Blue eyes just like his father's. Neil junior, Neil Blaine Kiser, and it suddenly hit her that she was no longer just an adulteress, but possibly a home-wrecker too. And yet, the warmth of his skin against hers was like heaven.

The house was haunted. From the frilly white curtains fluttering at a lone window, to the tubes of spermicide beneath the bed, to the floor of the bedroom littered with cardboard cartons overflowing with bras, slips, teddies, dresses and shoes, the spirit of Alicia lurked in every nook. No part of the house was free of her, except the basement. Alicia hated the basement. Everywhere else, Saro found she would have to exorcise the memory of Alicia, lazy woman, spoilt brat, voluptuous siren, compulsive shopper, selfish mother, errant wife.

Saro cleaned the bathrooms, scrubbing the bath till it gleamed. She threw open the kitchen cabinets, tossing out the stuff long past expiry date and arranging the rest with military precision. She loaded the temperamental washing machine and thwacked it till it began to hum. She put a stew on the stove to simmer, added a few herbs and left it there to cook in its juices till dinner time. She gave Blainey carrots to eat, washed his neck and behind his ears, tucked him into bed and read stories to him till he fell asleep. Then she collected the mounds of toys that lay on the floor beside his bed, and dumped them all into a giant wooden box that stood in the corner. And in the evening, when they all sat down to dinner, she watched them eat with a secret sense of accomplishment. Seven of them. Neil. Wolf and Maria, his girlfriend. Nancy, Wolf's mother, and Ben and Tom and Lisa—god knows who they were.

As they tore the crusty bread and dunked it into the stew, Alicia crept into the room.

'Blainey's been good all day,' Nancy said. 'When Alicia's here, he's forever throwing tantrums,' she explained to Saro.

'It's a miracle you've caused in here,' Ben mumbled. 'Alicia didn't know a thing about keeping the house clean.'

'Alicia just liked to dream of white picket fences and the lace curtains she would have in her home,' Maria broke in.

'Which meant we would have had to leave. She resented us.' Wolf's bitterness stilled the words.

And then Neil began harshly, 'My father used to beat up my mom for not tidying up the house. And it wasn't half as bad as this. She told me if I got a proper job and went to work in a suit and got rid of everyone here, we could be a family. And that she would cook and clean and be a proper wife.'

'So, where is she now?' Saro's voice cracked the wake of Alicia's absence.

Tom looked up from his plate. 'Didn't you know? They are having a trial separation.'

And Lisa tossed the hair off her face and asked, 'Anyone for coffee?'

In one of the cardboard cartons Saro found a faded rosebud and a letter. Neil's letter to Alicia, dated some weeks ago. She read and felt a lump lodge in her throat. And a strange sense of embarrassment, as if she had intruded on something private and sacred between two people.

Last night, after dinner, they had walked down to a bar. And Neil had talked of Alicia again. 'I never wanted to marry her. She was okay for a good time, but we had nothing in common. Then she got pregnant. And my mom got into the act. Between the two of them they wouldn't let it rest till we became man and wife.

'Do you know how we got married? I was piss drunk one night and when the two of them began to nag, I said, let's go, let's get married. So we drove into Virginia, knocked at the door of a Justice of Peace in some little town, and he proclaimed us married till death do us part.'

Saro looked at her feet. What was she supposed to say? Was she supposed to console him saying, don't worry, things will get better soon? She'll come back, you just see. Or, was she to say, forget her, I'm here for you? Wisely, she said nothing. Instead, she tried to describe her relationship with Sushil and found she couldn't. He seemed so far removed. Another life away, which she linked with every morning for a few minutes, murmuring inanities.

'Do you see that star? Right by the moon. Anytime you feel like slitting your wrists, just look at the sky and remember we sleep under the same star,' Neil had said, gazing down into Saro's eyes. And she had felt tears wet her cheeks and a vice clamp her tongue.

She crumpled the letter. Where had all his love for Alicia gone? Or was it Alicia who went away? What was more powerful? The witch's love pellet or Alicia's unwillingness to compromise?

Saro threw the letter and the rose into the carton, stuffed Alicia's underwear back and left the room. She didn't feel like cleaning up after someone else's mess any more.

Saro came down the corridor and paused to look at the picture Nancy made in the living room. She sat in a straight-backed chair, dressed in the moss-green velour robe she wore all day long, her lank grey hair brushing her hips, feet crossed at the ankles, hands resting limply in her lap, eyes staring into the leaping flames. What does she think about all day, Saro wondered.

'Hi,' she said softly, not wanting to startle her from her reverie.

Nancy turned her head. 'Hi.' She smiled. 'Come, pull up a chair.'

Saro dropped to her knees and sat on the pile carpeting that had worn thin in spots. She leaned against the couch and watched the flames throw dancing shadows across the walls. 'Until I came here, I'd never seen a fire in a fireplace,' she said. 'It's fascinating.'

Nancy smiled enigmatically at her and Saro thought, she's not all there.

'When I was blind, I used to sit by the fireplace and let the fire warm my eyes,' Nancy said as she began braiding her hair.

'When Wolf was a baby, my sister used to babysit him for me. One day I came home from shopping to find her in bed with my husband. I don't remember what I felt. Betrayed, hurt, devastated. All I knew was I felt this terrible rage gather within me, until it turned my fingers into talons and my fists into hammers. I ripped. I tore. I smashed everything that came in my way. I think I destroyed everything there was in that house. I had to be sedated before they could take me away. And when I woke up, it was to a black vacuum. The doctor said I had hysterical blindness.'

Saro twisted the gold band around her finger. Why was she telling her all this?

'Have you decided what you're going to do with your life?' Nancy asked. 'You don't want to just fill a void, do you?'

'He loves me, Nancy.'

'He's in love with you,' Nancy said gently. 'There's a

difference. The two of you have nothing in common. How long is it going to be before you tire of him? Think about it.'

Saro pulled her knees to her chin. Right now, everything about Neil delighted her. She liked the way he whistled under his breath. She smiled indulgently when she found him reading Danielle Steele. She watched him fondly when he rolled a joint. Most of all, she sighed in ecstasy when he made love to her. But was it going to be enough? Who cares, she decided recklessly. When she surfaced from her thoughts, she was alone in the room. Nancy had gone back to her room. So she went in search of Neil.

She went down to the basement, not sure if Neil wanted her there. 'Hi Saro.' Ben waved her to sit beside him. 'Do you have cable in India?'

'We didn't, but we do now.' Saro smiled.

'Cool. So you've seen *Friends*. Love that show. Do you?' Ben asked anxiously.

'Yeah.' She grinned.

'Do you get dope there?'

'I guess so. Why?'

Ben looked at her from beneath his lashes. 'Maybe I want to move down to India.'

'Maybe you should,' Saro offered. 'And bring Neil with you.'

'Why do you need him when you've got me?' Ben whined plaintively.

'You're not grown up enough for me. You like sugarpops and the Simpsons,' Saro joked, tugging at Ben's hair.

'So does Neil,' Ben grumbled.

'He does?' Saro asked in surprise. And then caught Neil looking at her and forgot all her doubts in her desire for him.

'Come here, woman.' He wagged a finger at her, and like Boy, she curled at his feet and let him twine his fingers through her hair.

She didn't understand what it was about him that inflamed

her senses. When he'd pulled out a shotgun from under the bed, she'd felt the cold metal on the palm of her hand as smooth as his silken skin. 'If somebody ever comes to get me, I want you to use this to help me escape,' he had said, showing her how to push down the trigger. 'Don't worry about aiming, just put your finger here and pull it back.' And she who had to grit her teeth and clench her heart to kill a cockroach, nodded her willingness. For him, she was ready to draw blood, shatter bones or rip flesh.

With the memory of the menacing barrel, the last piece fell into place. Alicia's resistance to this commune, the blossoming of spirit in the basement, the whispers into the telephone, the money that was waved in fistfuls without anyone seeming to work for it, the wolfhound that was meant to go for the throat, and the shotgun. She thought of Nancy's face as she said, 'You have nothing in common.' Neil dealt in drugs and yet, she knew she would forgive him even that.

What she couldn't forgive though, was the douche he'd gifted her the first evening.

'What's this?' she'd asked eagerly, pulling open the wrapper.

'I want you clean. Untouched,' he'd said, sitting on the bed. She'd dropped the half-open package on the bed and turned to him fiercely. 'What do you mean, untouched? I've never done this before. Just because I'm here doesn't mean I do it with every other man!'

'I didn't mean that.' Neil was contrite. 'I wanted to pretend that you are mine and no one else's. I wanted to forget you are married.' And then he began kissing her and when he pushed her into the bathroom and handed the douche to her, she did exactly what he wanted. She returned to his arms clean, untouched, almost virginal.

In the early hours of the morning, he woke her up and said, 'Honey, put some clothes on. Do you mind sleeping the rest of the night on the living-room couch? Blainey's going to be upset if he sees you in his mommy's place.'

Wordlessly, Saro had pulled her clothes on and gone to sleep on the couch. She'd curled into a ball, shoved her fists into her mouth and wept her heart out.

And now, crouched at his feet, it was this memory that returned to bruise her love for him. Never mind that next morning Neil had made up: he'd picked her up in his arms and carried her outside and threatened to drop her in the snow if she didn't smile at him. She'd giggled and forgiven him his insensitivity of the night before.

Was she just filling a void? He was besotted with her, but it was a soulless attraction. After all, the witch had only promised her power. But after five days of power, she wanted more. She wanted to matter to him.

The bong was a blue tube of glass, fragile and potent. Saro lay on the carpet and watched it move around the basement, from hand to hand. Blainey was asleep. He was not allowed to come down into the basement. At his playgroup they often showed the children pictures of pipes and needles and asked them if they'd seen things like these before, and if yes, where? 'So we are very careful when Blainey's around,' Neil said.

All day long she had watched Blainey stare out of the window restlessly. He often asked for his mommy and she consoled him that his mommy would come back soon. And strangely, as she said the words, she believed them to be true. When his eyes began to droop, she fed him a peanut-butter grape-jelly sandwich, bathed him and tucked him into bed. By the time she finished reading him a story, he was asleep. When she was gone, she hoped he would miss her and think of her once in a while.

The bong had floated across the room several times but when Saro asked for it, Neil was uncertain. 'Are you sure?'

'Yes, I'd like to know what it feels like.'

He lit it for her and she pulled the smoke in till it filled her lungs and wreathed itself around her mind. She felt the fist within that had hurt her all day uncurl, tiny wings sprout on her heels, and a lassitude streaked with narrow bands of relief descend upon her. She smiled at Neil and reached for his hand.

He peered into her eyes and asked angrily, 'Is this what I am to you? An experience? Did you want to know what it feels like to fuck a white man?'

'Ssh...ssh...' she soothed. 'I am black, but comely,' she quoted. 'Look not upon me, because I am black, because the sun hath looked upon me: My mother's children were angry with me; they made me the keeper of the vineyards; but mine own vineyard have I not kept. Tell me, O thou whom my soul loveth, where thou feedest, where thou makest thy flock to rest at noon: for why should I be as one that turneth aside by the flocks of thy companions?'

'Wow!' Neil exclaimed. 'Are you high, babe?'

'A little,' Saro said. Just enough for me to view our situation objectively, she said to herself. She rose and raised her hands. 'Adieu friends, it's been nice knowing you.' As she walked up the stairs, she heard them snicker.

When Neil lay down beside her, she drew him to her with an urgency bordering on desperation. She caressed his mouth, his cheeks, his eyes, his flanks, and from the recesses of her mind rose the words of a song written thousands of years ago. A song as pagan as the intensity of her need for him. She drew his hair to her breasts softly, breathing: 'My dear one is dazzling and ruddy, the most conspicuous of ten thousand. His head is gold, refined gold. The locks of his hair are date-clusters. His cheeks are like a garden bed of spice, towers of scented herbs. His lips are lilies, dripping with liquid myrrh. His abdomen is an ivory plate covered with sapphires. His legs are pillars of marble based on socket pedestals of refined gold. His palate is sheer sweetness and everything about him is altogether desirable.'

Soft, sibilant whispers swirled through the air, filling the space between them until his tongue darted into her mouth, drinking deep of her love, and she rejoiced in the sweetness of the suck. She wanted to feel him on every inch of her body, allow him entry into every crag, crevice and concealed part of herself. And so he loved her with an abandon that was almost demoniac in its insatiable appetite. Through the night, until the day began to breathe and the moon had fled, she allowed him to shepherd his lust among the lilies of her want. At last, when he was spent, she lay with her head on his chest and once again through her echoed the song, 'This is my dear one, this is my boy companion.' But because she knew the time had come to break the spell, to stop filling a void, she chose to say, 'I love you.'

Some minutes later, when she looked into his eyes, she saw the whites of his eyes glisten in the pale light of the room. 'Honey,' he mumbled, 'Alicia called. She wants to come back.'

'When do you want me to leave?' Saro asked quietly. Strangely, she didn't feel hurt. It was as she'd expected it to be. There was nothing left to say or do. He was no longer hers.

'First thing in the morning, I'll put you on a Greyhound.'

She could hear the relief in his voice. What had he expected? That she would raise her voice, shed tears and refuse to go away? Saro closed her eyes and pretended to sleep.

In the morning, Ben and Neil drove her to the Greyhound stop. In the car, when she sneezed and mumbled, 'I'm sorry,' Neil snapped, 'Don't say sorry. Say excuse me.'

She stared at the back of his head for a moment. And decided that her place in his life would be in a cardboard carton stuffed with odds and ends, relegated to some forlorn corner of his memory.

The Greyhound filled and began to move. She kept her head straight. She didn't want to turn and see that they had left before she had.

She drew the pouch out of her bag and held it in her hand like a talisman. She hadn't lost anything that was irretrievable.

In the seat next to her sat an old woman with a scarf tied around her hair. Liver spots, puffy wrists and a crease-proof dress bunched at her knees.

She took out a pellet and put it into her lipstick case. It would be a kind of insurance if Sushil ever found out about Neil. Meanwhile, she had one pellet left.

'Here, take this.' She offered the pouch to the old woman.

'What's in it?' the old woman asked suspiciously.

'The power to the world. Feed it to anybody, the President, the Pope or the plumber, and he'll be your slave. Make sure that you are the first person whose eyes he looks into, after you have fed it to him, and don't ever say "I love you" to him. For your power will evaporate just like this,' she said, snapping her fingers.

'Who are you?' the old woman asked, holding the pouch as if it contained a live snake.

'I am a witch,' Saro whispered, and closed her eyes.

When she opened them, the old woman had moved across the aisle to sit beside a young man wearing a baseball cap. He had a soft voice and seemed to have all the time to talk to an old woman. They were deep in conversation. Was she telling him about the strange encounter she'd just had? Was she losing her heart to him with every sympathetic nod he gave her? Would she try to see if the love pellet worked, Saro wondered. Slowly, she felt a laugh gather within her. Laugh, laugh, woman, she told herself sternly, if you don't, you'll cry.

As the bus rode through the sunrise, its insides were filled with a warm chuckling that dripped out and hung in the air, long after the bus had disappeared into the horizon.

the heart of a gerund

Grammar books are deceptive. Just open your mind and walk through the pages of one. You will be surprised at what you stumble across.

Unfairness, mostly. If you think the world is an unfair place, comparable to none, just remember this discrimination was created by a human hand. Not by laws of nature, economics or space.

As you pass by, you will see one article is assertive, definite, while the rest are a vacuous watery lot.

You will notice some vowels are rounded, while some consonants are sidelined.

You won't miss the parasites: the prefix and the suffix. Don't stay there too long or they'll attach themselves to you.

And then there is the gerund. Aching to be loved. Wanting to be possessed. Needing to be needed.

But don't let your heart bleed for her. The gerund doesn't like pity. The gerund has dignity. The gerund knows how to shut herself in. The gerund could be Norah, stuck in the grammar book of life.

'I am not like them,' I want to scream. But Sister Katherine doesn't like screaming either.

'Norah,' she says in that crisp voice of hers. 'We follow rules here. If we didn't, there would be chaos. You have to put your breakfast set away and use the steel plate and glass like everyone else does.'

Sister Katherine of the starch-board bosom and craggy face is the warden for the floor. She carries soup in bowls to the invalids and spoons it into their mouths with the deftness of a machine. In out, in out, with never a drop spilt, dribbled or spat out.

She wakes us up in the morning. Gives us a cup of weak tea. Those of us who know the taste of better tea hate it and yet, we drink it gratefully. It prods our eyes open. It does things to our nerves. It stirs our bowels and gives us enough reason to get up from our beds every morning.

Then comes breakfast. Idli, upma, oats and, once a week, pancakes. Food for the babies and the old. Food that doesn't require any effort to eat.

'All of us are not lucky enough to have dentures like you, Norah.' Yet another homily from Sister Katherine to troublesome Norah.

She treats us like children, leading us from one mealtime to the other. From dawn to dusk. From one day to another.

I sit here in the white-painted cane chair and watch the minute hand of the clock crawl on the face of time. There is little else to do.

When Mummy died, my life seemed to fall apart. Lennie in Kolar and Maxie in Cochin pleaded, 'No space for you, sis. Sorry.' When Mummy died, the pension stopped coming. The rent had to be paid. The bills overflowed the mailbox. Electricity. Groceries. My nerves cracked up.

When I recovered, the parish priest paid me a visit. He

suggested I come here. He didn't say I had nowhere else to go. Nobody did. So it was a decision I made.

I sold Mummy's furniture. There was hardly anything; the boys had carted them away when I was ill. I gave our books to the Catholic Club and packed a suitcase with a few odds and ends. Things I'd had for a lifetime and needed to have around me, no matter where I was. An Edward VIII Coronation breakfast set. (Poor Teddy, the coronation that never was.) A silver spoon. A porcelain cat. The family album. Mummy's Bible bound in real leather and of course, all my clothes.

It wasn't easy pulling the door shut, locking it and walking away. But what else could I do?

A month ago, I was Norah Webber.

Now I'm inmate No. 62, destined to live my life out among the senile and destitute. I am not like them. They were sent here; I came here.

Sister Katherine doesn't understand the difference. To her, we are all the same.

The bell rings. It is a huge bronze bell with a peal that reverberates into the farthest room.

Sebastian, the bell-keeper, is seventy years old. He used to be a watchman, a long time ago. Now he rings the bell to announce a visitor, a stranger, anyone passing through the gates.

Sometimes he manages to get their attention. He asks them questions he has no business asking. He delays them with quips, queries, instructions and inanities. He is a lonely man, Sebastian.

The notes of the bell ring in my ears. Ding dong, they go like the clock in Mummy's parlour.

But oh oh, what is this?

Bulbs pop, lights flash and through the haze of confusion, I hear Sister Katherine say, 'Now, now, don't work yourself into a state. All he did was to take a photograph of you.'

I can hear my heart beat as they walk away. I press my hands to my lap to stop them from trembling. I start rocking. The rhythmic creaking of the cane chair soothes me. It always has. I think of pleasant things. Like my breakfast set.

The lovely set with the picture of Edward VIII on it. I've had it for so long and now, they won't let me use it. Mummy was the same. 'No, Norah, it is much too valuable. Put it back into the cabinet right now.' She didn't even like me holding it.

I can see it on a tray laid out with an embroidered cloth. Buttered toast on the plate, a soft-boiled egg nestling in its cup. A bowl filled with cornflakes. And a cup with strong Lipton tea.

But Sister Katherine won't let me. 'No, Norah, we can't have toast and eggs for breakfast. It's too messy.

'No, Norah, you have to use the same kind of plates the others do. The maids here can't be responsible for your china. I can see it is valuable. Give it away or do what you want. But don't leave it lying around.'

I get up and go into the dormitory. My bed is by the window. The window has a huge sill. I lay the set out on the ledge.

Devi comes and stands by my side. She picks up the egg cup and peers into it.

It has been explained to me that Devi suffers from dementia. Her clock is stuck at twelve. In her mind, she is ten years old, waiting for her father and brothers to come home before she can serve herself any food. Devi is always hungry. She has flashes of lucidity, but they don't last.

At first, the family she was working for found it strange but amusing. Devi had been working for them for over forty years. Then it became embarrassing watching a seventy-nine-year-old woman cavorting like a twelve-year-old. So they found a place for her here.

Devi walks away with the cup. I don't protest; I don't know why. Suddenly nothing seems so precious any more.

I hear something smash. King Edward-who–never-was-king smashed to smithereens. I giggle.

'Look what you've done,' Sister Katherine fumes. 'I told you not to leave it around. I can't be responsible for everyone all the time.'

I look up. Tears run down my cheeks. She thinks I'm crying. 'I am not crying,' I assure her.

'I am not upset at all. You are right, as always. Just like Mummy was. I'll never leave it lying around again.'

One by one, I pick up the pieces of the set and delicately drop them to the floor.

This one's for you, Mummy, for never letting me use your precious china.

This one's for you, once more, Mummy dear, for making me dust it every day of my life, only to tell me, 'Darling, Lennie's the one who'll inherit it. He's my oldest, my heir.'

This one's for you, big brother Lennie, for thinking you'd inherit it just because you happened to be born first. You never knew that I had hidden it away as soon as Mummy died. You didn't know what happened to it, did you? I saw your fox-faced wife looking for it.

Ping. Ting. Ping. They shatter and shard.

Sister Katherine is aghast; Mummy, too. But Mummy is dead, so why is she standing beside Sister Katherine?

I think I'm going mad.

I let her push me back onto the pillow. I allow her to run her fingers through my hair. My eyes feel heavy. My mind is listless.

She croons, 'Hush, hush.'

As I drift off, I think, in those linear contours there is gentleness too.

Some time has passed since that day. Was it a month or two months ago, I don't remember. I can't even remember what I ate two days ago.

The bell rings. Sebastian died a while ago. He fell asleep one night and never woke up. The new bell-keeper is Naidu. Unlike Sebastian, he is a taciturn creature. He hates children, dogs, strangers, everybody.

He had a good job. When he retired, he used up all his money to build a house. He was a widower, so he invited his daughter and her husband to stay with him. He bequeathed the house to his grandchild.

After that they had no use for him. In many different ways they made their resentment clear. Until he asked them, begged them to send him away. Anywhere.

Naidu turned against people after that. He quarrelled with everybody at the home. The sisters grew so tired of restraining him that when Sebastian's slot fell vacant, they gave it to him gladly. He sits in his little hutch there, glaring at the world, transforming his hate into bell-notes every time someone walks in through the gate.

Polly cocks her head and cackles. She lives in a cage on the veranda. Like most of us here, Polly talks to herself. After some time, it doesn't matter if there isn't anyone to hear what we have to say. It is enough to speak, to air your woes, mutter grievances…

I start as someone taps my shoulder. Sister Katherine and a stranger. He smiles. She says, 'Congratulations, Norah!'

She sees the question in my eyes. 'Don't you remember him taking your photograph? Well, your photograph has won him a national award. He's won twenty thousand rupees and he's donating every rupee to our fund.'

I smile at him. He's ugly. Short, stocky and sallow. His eyes bulge. But when he smiles, it is with his whole being. I decide he seems alright.

Sister Katherine pats me on my back and walks away. He doesn't. He continues to stand there.

'What can I do for you?' he asks softly. I look up. What can he do for me?

'Oh, I don't need anything here. But thank you.'

'No, there must be something,' he insists.

'Will you... will you come in and talk to me once in a while?' It pops out before I can stop it.

He reaches out to take my hand. I like the feel of my palm in his. His stubby fingers exude a certain warmth. Suddenly, the crinkled dry, papery skin of my hand feels like a young girl's. Delicate. Soft. And smooth. I would like this moment to last forever.

Sister Katherine comes out onto the veranda where I sit with the young man. 'Would you like to join us for lunch?' she asks.

He nods.

We go to the dining room. There are rows of long tables with chairs. Most of us can still feed ourselves. For once, the food doesn't smell like vomit.

I can feel the young man's eyes dart, taking in everything. I try to see us as he must see us.

I see old men and women cramming food into their mouths. Slobbering, dribbling, splattering crumbs. I see the shaking hands and toothless mouths. I see the greed in the eyes.

I stand up, unable to watch him watching us. 'I need to go. I don't feel too well. Excuse me, excuse me,' I say, as I push my chair back.

Sister Katherine's eyes follow me to the door. But I keep going.

The young man visits me every Saturday afternoon. The first time, he brings me a box of cream cakes.

Sister Katherine doesn't like gifts of food. She must have said something, because he never brings me any cake again.

But he brings me other things. A pair of slippers. A bar of lavender soap. Magazines, and even a pashmina shawl.

I don't know what we talk about. For an hour, every week, he sits by my side, talking, joking, listening, sharing. Making me feel like the most wanted person on earth. And for the rest of the week, memories of that hour alleviate my loneliness.

I reminisce about that hour. Plan tidbits of conversation for the next time. Work myself into a state of nervous excitement until he walks in.

I am sitting on my bed, thinking of interesting things to say to him when Narsamma comes in, clutching a candy ball in her grimy paw. She is a little senile. She calls me 'Missy' and tags after me. She presses the candy ball into my hand and says, 'Eat it. I saved it for you.' She doesn't stop saying it until I do.

I put it into my mouth where neither tongue nor cheek will have anything to do with it. I heave. I think I am going to throw up.

Then Narsamma says, 'Missy, your photo is on the noticeboard.'

I swallow the candy ball in my surprise. Then skip up the veranda and across the quadrangle, skirting the chapel and flowerbed, to stand in front of the noticeboard.

It is a clipping from a newspaper, with a photograph of a woman. Straggly hair. Wrinkles. Lines and blotches. Eyes vacant. Hands that are tying and opening knots in a handkerchief. He hasn't missed a thing. Even the liver spots.

It is the portrait of an old woman. The study of a destitute old woman with no place to go and nothing to do.

An old woman who sits shrouded in loneliness, mumbling to herself.

I stumble back to my cane chair. My legs are shaking.

I began to rock, watching the crows swooping in and out. The crows are not scared of us. All we can do is flail our arms helplessly. Even the crows know that.

I feel betrayed. I feel ugly. I feel old and lonely and know there is nothing I can do about it. Except maybe shut the image out of my mind.

When Sister Katherine comes out to feed Polly, I say, 'Sister Katherine, I don't want that young man visiting me any more.'

She raises her eyebrows. 'But why? He is your only visitor. I thought you were fond of him.'

'He asks too many questions. He tires me out with his talking. He wants to know about Mummy, my brothers. And then, when he's gone, they come back to haunt me. My head starts hurting, my heart beats faster...' I start to cry.

Sister Katherine keeps patting me on my back, but I can't stop crying.

I lie on my bed and stare at the ceiling. The sun finds its way through the window bars and dapples the floor. The other three people in the room are asleep.

It is a Saturday. A Saturday afternoon.

The bell rings.

I close my eyes. A lifetime later, I hear footsteps down the corridor. They stop near my window.

If I reach out, I'll be able to touch him. I can smell his cologne. I can hear him breathe. I can feel the beat of his heart. I can sense the pity he has for me.

He looks at me for how long I don't know. Then he walks away.

When the footsteps fade into the distance, I open my eyes. And close them again.

I try to sleep. What else is there for me to do?

mistress of the night

Six o'clock. There is about this time a certain weariness. An intensity of grey that makes a man feel life is passing him by and that there is no way he can control what is happening to him. He is helpless, for how can he prevent the thickening of his arteries or the clouding of his eyes? As he clings to the subway strap, his knees twinge and he thinks how, after a shower, it isn't so easy any more to raise his legs and wipe his feet. And as he loops his belt around him, the spread of his once trim waistline is a reminder of looming mortality.

6 p.m. When cars sprout eyes and angular structures contort into softened shadows. When faces become mysterious and open windows lit from within frame a tableaux of content. Freeze that moment. Now turn and seek the sky. Don't gasp in shock when you see the clouds smeared with bruises. It's the aftermath of having survived the day. Purple blotches that indicate all is not magical about this hour.

As the evening approaches, I drive home feeling wrung out. I used to take the subway home. Not any more. I feel I must keep close to my means of escape. A sense of dissatisfaction curdles within me. I don't like this creature I've become. Often I wish I could change lanes, ignore the lights, get onto the highway and just keep going till I find some answers, some understanding as to why I was put on this earth.

As each evening fades, I am where I usually am. On the couch, with whisky sloshing in a tumbler. Five years ago, I thought I had stumbled upon the meaning of life when the estate agent showed me the house. Three-quarter of a million dollars and the house is yours, he said. I didn't have that much money, but I had a very good credit standing and I fell in love with the house. No, love is the wrong word to describe my feelings for the house. It was a passion, a need to possess, to lay my stamp on its every nook and cranny. And in the manner of a man obsessed by a passion, I let the house rule my every thought.

The house was a wanton, flagrantly demanding but appreciative when I gave myself to it wholly. When I stripped the ugly green paint off the woodwork, I discovered original oak. The tiffany glass was shrouded in grime and neglect. A painted-over door in the kitchen revealed a dumb waiter stricken with autism. The huge porcelain baths had clawed griffin feet wrought out of brass, but wreathed in green paint.

It was as if the previous owners had wanted to obliterate everything that was noble and exquisite about the house under a layer of regulation but democratic green. I was a man with a cause. A vision. A dream. And it kept me going. I didn't question the merit of each day I was living through. But then, passion becomes less intense with time and soon there was little left for me to do. Or even if there was, I was no longer driven by the desire to restore and embellish. It seemed to me that I had outgrown the confines of the house.

Every evening I sit on the couch flicking channels. I don't know what I am looking for. Sometimes a word or a picture or even a title grabs me and I pause. But mostly I run through all the channels before I settle on something my wife and I can view without taxing our minds. She sits on a wing chair upholstered in the same Fortuny fabric as the couch. The fireplace is no longer in use. Instead, the grate is filled with the blaze of chrysanthemums. On the mantelpiece is her collection of ivory figurines and at our feet are the dogs. My wife is talking. She is telling me what she's planned for the evening meal (it's Tuesday, so it ought to be broiled Cornish hen with broccoli in cheese sauce and steamed rice for me); for our vacation to Venice in three weeks' time; for the Memorial Day Weekend barbecue party we throw every year... she's planned and charted the course of the rest of our lives.

I stare at the woman I have been married to for the past fifteen years and I realize we have nothing in common. There is nothing about her that stirs my heart. I feel a tear at the back of my eye... What is happening to me, I wonder.

I get up and place the glass on a coaster.

It occurs to me then how much I have turned into a creature governed by the force of habit. I do things the right way. Only, it seems that in the process I have lost the ability to feel. To be spontaneous, warm and human. Right now I could be a humanoid going through the motions of living.

I pick up the glass and set it on the polished surface of the china cabinet. I wait for a moment and lift the glass once more. The ring it's left behind gives me a perverse pleasure. My wife frowns. I'm taking the dogs out, I tell her. She continues to frown. I walk down the steps unhurriedly. The dogs follow, their nails making a click-click sound on the wooden staircase. I look up the stairwell from the anteroom and then pat the dogs. Good girls, stay, stay, I say. I shut the door behind me softly, step out into the street and merge with the twilight. I switch my mobile off.

The park crouches in the middle of the city, a predatory beast, slumbering. In the hazy light, the tops of the trees wave menacingly. Suckers of the giant beast, they scan the skies for prey. A flock of birds screams and escapes into the horizon. A lone bird is grabbed and gobbled by the hungry mouth of the park. I sit under a tree and will my thudding heart to calm. This is New York, remember? Have you forgotten about that jogger who was raped in daylight? In every bush and stone crop, there is a violent creature lurking. Psychopaths and murderers. Muggers and junkies. I tell myself, if I can survive the night, I can survive anything.

I lie down on the bench with my hands cradling my head. It is early summer and not yet too muggy. Through the canopy of the branches, I catch a glimpse of the sky. A faint thread of light weaves itself through the dense stillness of the evening clouds. The park is slowly emptying. Children and balls are being gathered, dogs whistled to, lovers' trysts broken. Nannies wheel prams and charges home. I wonder if my wife has called the police yet.

I am wrapped in a great balloon of serenity. Nothing can dent it except the noisy cheeping of the birds as they settle for the night. Strangely, I feel a void. Something is not in its place and when I realize what it is, I feel homesick. Not for the townhouse on the Upper West side, but for home that is miles away. The jade coast, a besotted poet had called it. I close my eyes and embark on an astral trip. I am in the home of my childhood. My mother is there. My long-dead mother. We sit in the open courtyard like we always did in the evenings; she is singing softly, a song about Krishna. Night falls dramatically, the way it does in Kerala, and my balloon expands to absorb the music of the make-believe cicada. Suddenly, in every bush and stone crop, I now have a companion.

When I open my eyes, there is a woman sitting at the foot of the bench. She is brushing her hair, softly humming to herself. My arms feel stiff and my back hurts. I sit up and growl at the woman, 'Who the hell are you?'

She stares. 'Who would you like me to be? The she-devil, the flower princess, Zelda, or the mistress of the night? Can't you make out who I am, shit-head?'

She turns away and takes a compact from a fake leather bag. Then she draws out a tube of lipstick from the bag that seems to double as her vanity case. She opens the compact and with great dexterity, she paints her lips a silver mauve. She closes the compact with a snap, and drops it back into her bag along with the lipstick. Then she holds up her hands and examines them in detail. Next she brings out a nail file with which she gives her nails a quick once-over. She has nice hands, shapely and slender. In the fading light her skin takes on a pearly hue. She stands up, straightens her purple mini and begins to walk away.

'Don't,' I say softly. She stops and turns to look at me. Her face is bathed in shadows. The fragrance of jasmine goes up my nostrils with the speed of a line of coke. I am filled with a great yearning for home with its jasmine bushes that scent the night. 'Do you do this deliberately?'

'Do what?' she asks.

'Wear jasmine.'

'Honey, where are you from? It's not jasmine. It's perfume. Magie noire, ever heard of it?' she giggles.

'What do you think? Of course I have. Do you wear it deliberately? Magic of the night and all that?' I ask. I feel vicious and don't care who my victim is.

She stares at me for a long moment. I can almost see her mentally shrug off the desire to slam the bag in my face and run. She plasters a smile on her face. 'Gee, you sure have a lot of questions. But I have to go. I have work to do. Got to eat! Anyway, shouldn't you be going home too? What is a nice Indian man like you doing here? Go home to wifey, will you? '

'How much do you want?' I ask. Something, a wave of anticipation, radiates through me. I haven't made an impulsive decision for so long that it feels exciting. Seize the moment and hang the consequences.

I see surprise in her eyes. 'It depends on what you want,' she says without any emotion. 'I am not your average 8th Avenue hooker. I don't come cheap.'

'You sure don't look like you belong on Park Avenue either,' I sneer.

'Look, Mister, I didn't solicit business. So I don't have to take any shit from you. If you want me to stay, you better tell me how much money you have.'

For twenty years I've been living in Manhattan. I'm a vice-president in an advertising agency. My peers look upon me as a man of stature. Pick any business magazine and you'll find me quoted. There's hardly a trace of an accent when I speak and this hooker wants to know if I can afford her. Bitch. Fucking whore. Just because the colour of my skin is brown. In my country, a creature like you wouldn't dare cross my path… Suddenly, I realize what my thoughts are leading up to. This is my country now and this is the way I've chosen to live. So if a hooker wants to know if I can afford her, I'll tell her.

'Hey Mister, you better make up your mind fast. I'm leaving,' her voice breaks in.

'I want you to stay with me all night,' I mumble. It is as if somebody else is doing all the speaking. Who is this man who's taking control?

I watch myself open my wallet and remove all the notes in it. 'This is all I have,' I say, handing over ten fifties and six tens to her. 'I hope it will do.'

Satyr of the Subway

'I suppose so,' she says grudgingly. 'Wait here. I'll be back,' she murmurs as she disappears into the night.

Maybe she won't come back. Maybe she realizes I won't go after her. I sit on the bench inhaling the fragrance of jasmine she's left behind.

Minutes later, I feel her sitting next to me. 'You're back?' I exclaim, not knowing if that is good or bad.

'Who are you?' she asks. 'Are you a cop?'

'Of course not,' I say. 'Here, take a look at this.'

I offer my business card to her.

She looks at it and then stares at me thoughtfully. 'I guess you are okay.' She waves her hand and I hear the snapping of dry twigs as someone walks away.

'Who was that?' I ask in surprise. I'd thought we were alone.

'My protector,' she says mysteriously, giving that faceless presence the combined aura of Batman and Conan the Barbarian.

'You mean your pimp?'

'Call him what you want, but he takes care of me. And if you were a cop, he would have helped me get away.'

'How would he have done that?' Curiosity gets the better of me.

'Are you sure you want to know?' she smirks.

'Yes,' I insist.

'He would have knifed you or beaten you to a pound of pulp,' she says without a trace of remorse in her voice. She probably sees the fear in my eyes, for she adds, 'But you don't have to worry, fancy man. Let's get out of here.'

I hold back. I don't want to leave the park. Suddenly it has become my sanctuary. 'I don't want to go anywhere, I want to stay here.' My voice takes on the petulance of a three-year-old's.

'You must be kidding.'

'No, I'm serious. I want to stay here. In the park.'

'Jesus, my place doesn't have roaches or fleas. It might not be the Waldorf, but it is clean and safe.' She tugs at my hand.

'I don't care if you are staying at the Waldorf. I am not stepping out of this park. And I paid you to stay with me. So you do as I want.' I sound curt even to myself. Is this how I am at work, I wonder. A pompous prick?

'Fine. But let's move from here.' She holds out her hand to me.

We walk hand in hand and as if on cue, the moon comes out to lead us into the heart of the park.

I pull at a tuft of grass. She sits beside me, her legs stretched out. Somewhere between the time we met and now, she has managed to get her tights off and the moonlight bathes her toes, making them seem aloof and pale, vulnerable and delicate. Blossoms of the night.

'You have jasmine buds for toes,' I whisper to her.

She smiles. 'You don't have to sweet-talk me. Remember you paid to use me as you choose. And anyway, I don't know what a jasmine bud looks like. So why are you so obsessed with jasmine? This is the second time you've referred to it.'

'Forget it,' I mumble. Her cynicism bothers me. I wish she would go away. I close my eyes. The stillness of the night is something I don't want to share. There is a slight breeze. A few yards away, a tree moans. This is beautiful. Why didn't I do this earlier?

I hum to myself, *I like New York in June, how about you?*

The rustle startles me. I open my eyes and find her kneeling in front of me. Languorously, her eyes not leaving mine, she slides the zip down. 'So, fancy man, let's get started. Don't you like me?' She gestures to her naked breasts, her stomach that curves gently into a fur-lined V at the top of her thighs, the flaunting lines of her buttocks. I turn away, embarrassed.

'What are you?' she taunts. 'You are not gay or impotent, are you?'

She pauses for a moment. 'Don't tell me, you are a virgin.' She begins to giggle.

I lay my hand on her mouth. 'Hush, hush!' I whisper as I trail a finger down the length of her body. Her skin rises up in goosebumps to greet mine. She sucks her breath in, holding herself taut, and closes her eyes. As her eyelids go down, I glimpse a ghost in her eyes. A strangely familiar ghost. The spectre that has been haunting me all evening.

I cup her face in my palms and gently rub the balls of my thumbs on her cheeks. 'Don't be so gentle,' she mumbles, her head drooping, 'you are making me cry.'

She lifts her head, the hard-as-nails look coming back into her face. She tosses her hair and stares at me. 'Aren't you getting undressed?'

'No.'

'Would you like me to go down on you?'

'No!'

'Have it your way. What would you like me to do first?'

'Here,' I say, pointing to her heap of clothes. 'Put those on and lie down next to me.'

'And then do what?' she questions warily.

'Nothing. Just lie down. Let's talk.'

'About what?' she probes.

'I don't know,' I murmur. 'I wish I knew. About life, maybe.'

A strand of her hair lifts in the breeze and brushes against my face. I trap it between my fingers. 'Hair... hair that has spirit; moving with confidence... embraced by the energy of the wind and sun. Luminous, resilient hair; finding form and texture in nature.'

'Wow, that is some good poetry.'

I smile at the sky. 'That,' I say, 'is a Paul Mitchell hair systems advertisement from a long time ago, and not poetry.'

'Is that what you do?' she asks.

I am filled with admiration for her. Never mind how much I put her down, or make her conscious of her inadequacies, she is unfazed. Some self-esteem. I envy her that.

'What are you doing here?' she asks gently.

'I don't know. Trying to find some answers.' I shrug.

'Like what?'

'I wish I knew. All I know is that every day is the same. It's like climbing the same mountain day after day, knowing very well what I am going to find at the top. A plateau that slopes down to a precipice. There is no going beyond that. It all seems so meaningless. Why bother to climb, why go through all that turmoil and struggle… do you understand what I am saying?' I try to explain as much to myself as to her.

'So?' She is relentless, this woman I have bought for the night.

'So I got tired of it and decided to walk away from my home, my wife, from it all,' I grind out through clenched teeth.

'You give up easily, don't you?'

'I don't give up easily. If I did, I wouldn't be where I am today. I have been living this life for over nineteen years and I am weary of it. My career, my home, I am so bored.'

'Does that include your wife?' she murmurs slyly.

'Sort of. I just realized we have nothing to say to each other except inanities.'

'I sure would have nothing to say to you if you used such big words all the time. Is this how you talk even to your dog?'

I grin. 'Not all the time, but mostly. But that's enough about me. Tell me about you.'

I know what she is going to ask next: So what will you do now? I don't know the answer myself. I don't know what I am going to do next.

She is pulling apart a leaf meticulously. The moon is shrouded by a floating cloud. When she sits up, her profile is pure. Her silvery mauve lips are full and luscious. Plums laden with nectar, fruit I discover I would like to feast on. She clears her throat once, then she becomes still. A sculpture hewn out of shadow. When she speaks, her voice takes on the hardness of granite.

'Every morning when I wake up, I think the day is going to be different. I pour myself a glass of orange juice, I nibble on a slice of toast, too restless, too excited. I can feel my destiny tugging me in a new direction.

'Then a man comes, and he pays to fuck me. And slowly the day begins to feel less wonderful. Yet another man comes and he wants me to take him in my mouth. Each time I think, this is the last one. The next one is going to be my Prince Charming. By the time the day is over, I have little energy left. So I go to sleep. And I wake up and I dream and I get fucked.'

I don't like her tone of voice. I can't stand the detachment in her words. She doesn't have to state it; I get the message. 'Are you trying to make me feel guilty?' I ask peevishly.

'Guilty about what?' She sounds genuinely baffled.

'For complaining about my gilt-edged life when yours seems so hopeless.'

'Look,' she says harshly. 'I wasn't asking for pity. I wasn't aiming to get you sobbing. Everyone is entitled to a dream. I was just telling you about mine. As for hopeless, how do you know that I am not a schoolteacher or a doctor or a salesgirl at Macy's who likes fucking around?

'You know what, I don't have to do this. And anyway, freedom is a very subjective feeling,' she adds casually, as an afterthought.

'Not bad for a whore. You are quite a philosopher, aren't you?' I want to see the smoothness of that visage crumble. I want to draw blood. How dare she make me feel like an inadequate worm?

She doesn't retaliate. She just lies there, her hands under her head, unmindful of the stains the grass would leave on her clothes.

For an old-time New Yorker, the silence is unnerving. Where are all the cop cars that go cruising with their whining sirens? Where are the jets that crisscross the skies with their steady drone? I feel cold and unhappy.

She turns on her side and looks at me. 'When you spend as much time as I do on my back, with my eyes closed, pretending ecstasy, the mind is free to wander.

'And we are not all that bad as—what did you call it— philosophers. We see you as you are. Your real self. Your fears and failings.

'Men with twisted minds. Men with broken souls. When they leave us, they go back healed for the moment, feeling complete and a little less tortured. Isn't that what a philosopher does? Make a person feel less confused, less troubled?' she asks with dignity.

I have always considered myself a compassionate man. And here I am hitting out to make myself feel better.

'I'm sorry.' I touch her arm.

'For what? You can call me names. You can even hit me if you want, as long as it's not my face. You own me for the night, remember?'

'Will you stop that? I don't own you. I don't want to hit you or hurt you.'

'What do you want?' she asks flatly. She is all planes in the moonlight. The grass prickles my back. I sit up, wanting to gather her in my arms. I am filled with a great surge of love for her.

'Help me find out. Live with me.' I hold her close, trying to communicate my need to her. 'You've made me look at myself. No one's ever been able to do that. Come with me. Let me be the direction your destiny has been pushing you towards.'

She laughs and pushes me aside. 'You must be kidding. Can you see me and you together? Besides, how do I know that in five years' time you won't get tired of me and start looking for a new cause?'

'Hey, hey,' I protest. 'Hold it there. I wasn't offering you suburban bliss. I was talking of a life together...'

'What does that mean?' she cuts in. 'Weekend tumbles and Wednesday afternoon meetings? No, mister, I know what I want.

'I want somebody who will put me first. See in me some truth he's been seeking all his life. I don't want a man looking for a cause to give meaning to his life. I don't want a man avenging himself on society by taking up with a whore. I don't want heroes or saints. And you are too wrapped up in yourself for my liking. In all this time we've been together, you haven't even asked me my name.'

'So, what is your name?'

'Why do you want to know?' she asks.

'So that when I think of you in the middle of the night, or when I'm feeling particularly maudlin, you are not just a face.'

She watches me from under her eyelashes, trying to discern if I am serious. 'Lisa,' she murmurs.

'Lisa,' I saw slowly, 'will you call me some time? You have my number. It is on the card I gave you. I would like to take you out for a drink, maybe lunch. That is, if you have the time.'

She smiles. 'That would be nice.'

'Hey,' she continues after a long moment, 'come here, give me a hug.' She draws me into her arms and cradles me against her bosom.

'You know what, life is not as bad as you think. We did find something here, tonight. Who would have thought of that?' she murmurs against my temple, running her fingers through my hair, willing me to close my eyes.

In the morning when I wake up, I am alone. Something glints in the faint light of dawn. My mobile.

I switch it on and call my wife. Come and pick me up, I say, a little contrite, a little abashed. In the clarity of the morning, I wonder what got into me.

As I wait for my wife, concocting a story to explain my absence, my lapse, I discover the card I had given her, in my pocket. The edges are a little bent and its face is stained. And from it comes a faint fragrance. I stare at it for a moment and put it back in my pocket.

the karmic cat

The cat uncurled. It stretched and flexed. Then it blinked.

Fish bones of sleep still clung to the cat. A queer kind of fatigue that rattled within his bones and hugged with the insistence of cankers. For a moment, the cat stared unseeingly. Then he allowed routine to take over.

He padded from his resting place to the grassy bank by the side of the road. Not too close. He'd seen what happened to cats who let their guard down on the highway. He'd seen cats skewered in mid-motion; cats splayed flat on the tarmac. Splattered cats, crushed cats, glassy-eyed, stiff-limbed, grimacing cats.

The cat sat on his haunches and licked around his lips. He was fastidious. If he had been a man, the cat's shoelaces would have been of matching length, his cheque foils filed, his face sluiced with water and soap several times a day.

The cat held his right paw up and licked it until it was damp. Then he passed his paw over his face and head, over and into his ear, across his eyes and down his cheek to his chin.

Not satisfied, the cat repeated the pattern with his left paw. Then he moved his attention to his shoulders, his flanks and legs. Convoluting himself, the cat finished washing his genitals before starting on the tail. From root to tip, the tongue moved. When it encountered a burr—there were several—the cat nipped at it with his teeth, delicately, expertly.

The cat as you see him now is no different from the two million and forty-three cats that inhabit the earth. All cats wash. Why, even the first Miacis created by the mysterious hand was known to wash, when not frisking between the feet of dinosaurs and mammoths.

One day, when the sheets of ice began to fall, the Miaci were buried in the fleecy cold that soon turned into an icy fist, holding down the slowly numbing Miacispirit in its frozen depths. When the organic forces next came together, some traits were new. And what finally emerged from a whisker, a tail, a paw, a purr, a disposition to wash and a savage enigma for a soul, was a being so complete that even in darkness it could see.

Tawny-felted, topaz-eyed, angel-hair-frilled, raspberry-tongued, this creation could be out of a fairy tale or a painting. The supine cat, content to sun itself on a wall speckled with moss and light, while a witless gecko clicked its tongue.

Not this cat. Seek his eyes. Peer into his mind, and maybe you'll get a glimpse of who he truly is. A cat that has never known restraint. A cat that has prowled in and out of the alleys of life, unwilling to be tamed by gestures of affection. So why then is the cat trying to attract attention?

'I have had enough of this life, this freedom as you call it. Try sleeping in the damp, night after night, not knowing what's for breakfast. A grasshopper or a squirrel? Try hunting for food, meal after meal. The endless chasing, the relentless searching…

'I want security. I want to wake up to a bowl of milk. I want to be indulged. I want to know what it feels like to shit in a tray someone else will rake, cover and clean. I want someone to worry if I stay out all night.

'Never mind if that someone wants to scratch under my chin. I'll allow that. I'll even purr in simulation of pleasure. I'll tell you what I'm prepared to do. I am ready to bury all the fierceness of spirit you seem to be so fond of celebrating, and settle down to being a house cat.'

The sky was a canopy of grey. A streak of lightning tore its fabric. Making this decision was hard for the cat. For, after all, he had decided to sell out. He did not despise the world, nor did he love it. He pitied it and knew that his chosen path would safeguard him from misery. The cat was willing to let his karmic forces steer him. The cat knew that years of concentration would stand by him, no matter how he chose to live the rest of his life. The cat was calm. The vibration of vehicles approaching from far away marked time. He knew for certain this would be the day. He waited.

She wanted to reach out and hold his hand. She wanted him to put his arm around her and allow his warmth to seep into her. She wanted him to do the one million things two people who loved each other were supposed to do. But he didn't. He just stared ahead, his hands moving automatically between the steering wheel and the gear. Change to second, then to third, fourth, so the minutes ticked by, and the windshield wipers continued to wipe the tears off the car's glassy cheeks. It was grey and clammy. She gnawed at her lower lip. Her teeth sinking into the soft flesh prodded her frozen heart with tiny flickers of pain.

He hardly saw the child anyway. An hour a day, maybe. She tried to make up for his neglect. She played games with him, fed and bathed him, and in the middle of a nightmare held him to her breasts, softly kissing his brow and running her fingers through his damp hair.

'You're spoiling him rotten,' he complained, waking up one night to find her coming from the child's room.

'Someone has to,' she snapped. It had been one of those weeks when he'd come home close to midnight, every night.

She'd waited all evening, glancing at the clock every few minutes. Starting at every footfall outside the door, telling herself it was him every time she heard the lift gates slam. Hating herself for being so vulnerable. For still being so much in love with him.

'I've arranged for his admission at the residential school,' he said one night, when she was lying on her side of the bed with her back to him.

'He will have to leave soon,' he added.

The rain continued to smear the glass. She couldn't get the picture of her child off her mind. He seemed so lost, so forlorn, waving as they drove away.

Suddenly she screamed, 'Stop!'

He slammed the brakes. He turned towards her furiously, but before he could say a word, she hurled herself out of the car.

When she returned, her face was streaked with the rain, her hair wet and her clothes damp. In her hands was a cat.

She opened the rear door of the car and got in. Without letting go of the cat, she pulled the bag closer and took a towel from it. Briskly, gently, she dried the cat.

Then she pulled her T-shirt over her head. She felt two pairs of eyes on her. A little abashed, she quickly slipped on a blouse.

'What was that all about?' he asked.

'I spotted the cat,' she said, brushing the rain out of her hair. 'He seemed so lost, so forlorn. It was as if the cat was waiting for someone. I think he was waiting for me.'

'Oh, great,' he said. 'Now we have a cat. I thought you said you were planning to go back to work...'

The cat raised its head and looked at the man.

The cat allowed himself to be held. It felt strange. Like the first time he'd climbed a tree.

He had stood in the crook of a branch and looked down. He hadn't realized he had climbed so high. He felt fear escalate through him. But then he let instinct take over.

He felt the warmth of contact. A pair of hands and a bosom. He shrank into himself. He squinted around him, seeking a way to escape from the confines of touch.

Hot air whistled through his ears as he fell through space. He sank into something so soft, so warm, he was sure he had attained cat nirvana. It was his first experience of comfort; of a cushion.

The cat lolled, allowing the softness to envelop him. Currant in a bun, pearl in an oyster, needle in flesh, a lash in the corner of an eye, a fly on a baby's bum. And, within him, the cat felt an intense affection for this square that had gathered him into its downy arms, cherishing him. A feeling so passionate that the cat knew he would kill to preserve it.

It was as if the cat sensed the vacuum between her and him. It was as if the cat wanted to fill the bleakness. Sometimes he sat on her lap with his face towards her, staring into her eyes. Topaz beads beamed love to her.

He was a cat like no other cat. He didn't weave his way between her legs or rub his face against her calves. He didn't arch his neck in pleasure when she scratched his back. Or even curl up at her feet. And yet, he liked to be as close to her as possible. She felt his eyes following her all day, drinking in the contours of her body. The power of his scrutiny stiffened the tips of her breasts to raisins, rustled her pubic hair and gripped her with a longing. Sometimes, as he watched, she let her fingers pluck at the fruit and then wander into the forest with the pull of a swamp. Later, her fingers smelling of her musky scent would slither across the trails that crisscrossed her abdomen. Make-believing the motions of a lover still enthralled by the newness of his passion for her.

And the cat would leap from where he lay, in the puddle of her clothes, on to her and peer into her eyes. No censure there, only approval and unconditional love.

The cat didn't understand himself. At first, she had just been there. The plumper up of cushions, the porter of filled bowls, the pipette of the mess he created.

When did that change?

Was it when her tears soaked his fur, or was it when she began talking to him, telling him all those things she told no one else? Or, was it when she shed her cloak of inhibition and allowed him to watch her seeking fulfillment with her fingers? Or, maybe it was when he noticed that she had stopped waiting for her husband to come home. Again and again, he searched her eyes for some sign. To see if she reciprocated the deep yearning he felt for her.

He sought her with a fierce possessiveness. With the ardency of a being who had chanced upon the truth of life and was afraid to blink lest it should go away.

He noticed. He observed. He watched. He chewed his lip. He narrowed his eyes. He cracked his knuckles. He felt his heart go into rigor mortis. He saw she was happy. And he saw that he was not the reason why she walked with a certain lightness of step and went through life with such cheeriness of tone.

Tantrums. Sulks. Tearjags. Blatant adoration. That's what he was used to. Not this woman who seemed fulfilled. A woman emotionally nourished, sensually satiated. A woman who made no demands on him.

He lay in their bed, listening to her even breathing as she slept. The cat nestled against her. The intruder in their bed, their lives.

What spell had this cat cast? When he walked into a room where they were, the cat stared at him, making him feel as if he had intruded upon a very private moment. The cat had perfected the art of shutting him out in his own home. It was them versus him.

Had the cat boiled together in a cauldron frog spawn and owl's eggs, fox's teeth and hyena spittle, nettles and lotus stems and seven kinds of herbs? Had he mumbled magic words over the bubbling contents of the cauldron? Had he strained the potion into a glass vial and applied it onto his pulse points? His temple, his throat, his testicles, his heart? How else had the cat lured her away from him?

He turned towards her and fitted himself into the curves of her inert body. He put his arm around her waist and drew her closer to him. He felt her melt into him. And within him began a singing.

The cat's ears stiffened. He felt the man move. He opened his eyes and saw the man's arm snake around her waist, hesitant at first, then confident, triumphant.

She was awake. Her senses were springing to life. The cat felt his hair stand on end.

He cringed at the desire he saw surge in her. Don't, he wanted to say, don't let him. He'll drink of your happiness and leave you hollow. All he wants is power over you.

The cat watched helplessly as the man rubbed his palms over her nipples. He looked on as the man nipped at her ear lobes, ran his tongue along the line of her spine and let his fingers maraud for treasure at the mound.

The cat knew he had a choice. To stay on and aggravate the pain. Or walk out of the room.

The bedroom was heavy with sexual malaise. The man assumed his position. She spread her legs to welcome him. Long time no see, let's catch up, what do you say?

The cat felt a sob choke him as their hips met.

The cat rose, radiating the hatred he felt. The cat wanted to fling himself on the man and sink his fangs into his skin. Tear through flesh, muscle and tendons, chew on his bones and drink his blood.

The cat felt betrayed, hurt and angry. He went to sit on his cushion and think.

'You don't treat the cat like a pet,' he accused.

'Of course I don't,' she gleamed in the darkness. 'How can I? He's hardly the kind of cat you can call kitty-kitty. He's got dignity. Do you see how he is? Aloof, detached. In fact, he reminds me so much of you.'

'That's the bloody problem,' he mumbled. 'He thinks he is your husband. Have you noticed how he looks at me? He treats me like I am the intruder.'

His fingers caressed the shirred satin of her belly. Boldly, she turned to him.

'Let's make love,' she whispered in his ear and slid her tongue into his mouth.

Once upon a time, the Great Master sat under a tree and thought. Millions of thoughts. Something yellow. Something red. Something white. A beam of light shining through a hole.

An outline of the world seen through a hole in a coin.

The top of the tree that moves with the wind. A bowl of clear water. A disc of clay. A constant flame.

The body. The breath. The inevitability of death.

Infinite space. Infinite consciousness.

And so the thoughts whirled, causing toes to tingle, heartbeats to accelerate. Suddenly a rogue thought moved away from the nervebed and found itself floating down an elusive channel. The single vein that runs from brain to heart to mind to soul.

And so potent was the power of this thought that he became the Enlightened One.

To exist is to suffer. Suffering has its roots in desire. Suffering can be escaped by elimination of desire. Desire can be overcome by discipline.

Once, the cat had sought the eight-fold path of discipline. Once, the cat had been free of desire. Once, the cat had known no suffering. Once, the cat had been just passing through.

Truth is an unruly spirit, and the truth about the cat is that he can no longer just pass through. He has let himself be diverted by the Evil One. Mara. Prince of darkness, ponce of temptation. His three nymphet daughters, Infatuation, Seduction and Sexual Love, have claimed the cat.

The darkness of illusion has clouded his mind.

The cat waited for the man to emerge. When he did, he saw triumph in the man's eyes. He saw the cockiness of victory. He smelt the scent of the woman's surrender.

And the memory of that musky fragrance that used to fill the air those other times spurred the cat into a frenzy. Gone was the aloofness of spirit, the detachment from desire. Gone was the infinite patience, the fullness of wisdom. One by one the cat shed the cardinal virtues so painstakingly cultivated and let his animal nature take over.

He hurled himself at the man, raking his claws across the bare chest she had kissed several times in the night with the lightness of a moth's wing.

He saw the man reel, the blood spurt, the scream start. He felt the man grab him and fling him across the room. He fell on his feet. Cats did that all the time. And yet, his anger wouldn't contain itself.

He leapt on the man again. This was a battle. Two men fighting a duel for the privilege of loving a woman. This was a battle, bloody and fierce, fought to be won.

The woman ran in, her long bare legs starkly pale in that room of shadows. She held the man to her, protecting him from whatever it was that was hurting him. The blood from his chest and face smeared her breasts and midriff.

'How could you?' she cried. 'After all that I've done for you, how could you?'

The cat felt a dull throbbing in his head. The man had won. She saw only the blood, the violence. She didn't see the pain, the hurt, the anguish within him.

She turned to help the man back to their room. She flinched at the angry scratches. Daubing cotton wool in warm water, she cleaned the wounds gently.

She nuzzled his neck with her cheek. 'I'm sorry you are hurt. I don't know what happened to the cat.'

'I told you, he is jealous. He hates me. Don't you see, he won't let us be. Get rid of him. If you want this marriage to have a chance, get rid of him.'

In the mirror, his eyes met the cat's.

The cat limped. He had a nasty wound on his hind leg. He ached all over.

The cat was miserable. The cat didn't know where he was going.

Satyr of the Subway

In the manner of the Great Master, the cat left the woman and the warmth she had meshed him in, seeking peace, seeking salvation for his bruised spirit.

The cat paused. His stomach heaved. Vomit dribbled out. The cat limped some more. He came to a tree that faced east. Beneath it was a mound of leaves. The rust and brown of the leaves stirred in him a flicker of loneliness. That first cushion had been fashioned out of such hues.

He sniffed the leaves. Crisp, dry and sunburnt. In the dappled shade beneath the tree, on the ground flecked with grass, the cat collapsed on a bed of leaves.

Slowly he allowed the tension coiled within him to unwind. Slowly, he let nothingness in. Something red. Something blue. A disc of clay.

When an existence disintegrates, the soul takes hold of a new location. Unfolding a life which is neither the same as the old, nor a new one, but the continuance of a series.

To exist is to suffer. Suffering has its roots in desire. Suffering can be escaped by elimination of desire and the need to possess. After all, we are all just passing through.

consider the tree

It stood in a damp patch of soil, squat, forlorn, mostly weary. The smaller branches had been snapped off and now tiny mounds of gnarled bark waved their stumpy fists in the air in mute rage. Beneath the ground was a jagged edge where the axe had spliced through, shredding the pith into a million fragments, snapping the tie that held together branch and trunk.

A grey-green branch with a patina of brown, three feet tall, trying to put out roots in a sympathetic heap of mud.

There had always been a drumstick tree in the periphery of my memory. The first one was a handsome tree that soared into the heavens from our back garden. Its trunk housed a rug of caterpillars that slithered into our nightmares so that we woke up scratching our arms and legs. And Mother would remark as she daubed antiseptic cream on our itching, burning skin, 'Didn't I tell you not to go near the drumstick tree?'

Once in a while, a man from my father's factory would come with a stick, one of its ends covered with rags, a bottle of kerosene and a box of matches. We would hover around and watch as he poured kerosene over the rag-end of the stick and set it ablaze. Holding it aloft, he would walk close to the tree and gently torch the swarming caterpillars until they turned into curls of carbon and fell to the ground.

When the tree trunk lay naked and exposed, we would carve

our initials into the bark with the sharp end of a nail, going back every day to freshen the wound and add a new one. Until the day the furred caterpillars came back, covering the gaping bruises and most of the trunk, taking the tree from our cruel hands to their soft woolly bosoms.

There were other trees too. Nondescript ones. Half-grown ones. Even the skeleton of a dead tree.

Once there was a young drumstick tree, forever peeping from my neighbour's yard into mine. Like a friendly puppy eager to make friends, it draped itself over the wall. A cascade of green that invited itself into my home. Some days, when the fridge lay barren and cold, I reached for its trusting arms and stripped them clean. The tree never held it against me. In a few days' time, it would be back again, demanding attention with its teardrops of green.

'But this one,' Amma had said as she planted it in the ground, 'was different. Everyone saw how lush its foliage was and as for those who tasted the succulence of its fruit...all of them wanted more. People snapped branches off the tree to plant in their gardens. Do you know it has so far resisted all such attempts at propagation?'

Yesterday, the first spike of green unfurled from one of the stumpy fists. Bashful as a young mother, it refused to meet anyone's eye all day long, preferring seclusion to company. This morning it seemed a little less shy. In fact, in keeping with the manner of a new mother, it held aloft its baby branches proudly. And so I stood there, pleading with it to live, willing it to survive.

'What's keeping you in the garden so long?' Amma asked, coming in search of me. When she saw the drumstick tree with its crown of leaves, she burst into tears.

The house was on a quiet road lined with old colonial bungalows and even older giant trees. A Rangoon creeper grew four feet away from the main door. And in the tiny patch that lined the front of the house stood a wispy pomegranate tree. I stood at the wicket gate and painted a picture of how I would transform this shabby old house into a quaint home. I was six weeks pregnant and still awed by the newness of the thought. Nothing was good enough for the baby until I had made it so.

Two days after we moved into the house, the milkman brought her along. I had wanted a smart young girl who would quickly pick up a smattering of English to handle telephone calls and open the door to visitors when I was busy, apart from dusting and cleaning and cooking a few meals. Later, when the baby was born, I wanted her to wheel her in a pram down the tree-lined avenue into the park.

'I don't think she'll be suitable,' I told my husband, thinking of the woman's stern eyes and the years on her face. I didn't want anyone who would tell me what or how to do things right. I didn't want her experience tainting my plans for the house and the baby. 'But I think I'll keep her till I find someone else.'

The next day I walked into the kitchen to hear glass splinter. One of the dessert bowls lay in slivers. 'Can't you be more careful?' I barked. 'Why don't you put the light on?'

I hoped she would leave without my asking her to.

The Rangoon creeper speckled with pink and white buds wreathed itself around the front door, filling the living room with its fragrance every evening. I snipped clumps of the delicate florets, added a few sprigs of foxtail asparagus and put them in a jar of water to keep in the kitchen. I wanted to make Amma's workplace sweet smelling and nice for her.

Satyr of the Subway

I don't remember how and when the transition took place. One day she was just the maid I kept on reluctantly. And then she became Amma. Mother. My mother. More beloved to me than my real one in so many ways.

The house had a backyard fringed with many trees. A half-wall separated the yard from the garden. On it I placed my many pots of begonia, verbena and Wandering Jew. Often I would sit there in the backyard, a cat at my feet, my hands resting limply on my gently swelling belly, secure and content in the knowledge that Amma was close at hand.

On one of those near perfect days, as I sat shelling peas and watching Amma fold the washing, I said, 'What I really feel like eating is drumstick-leaf curry. I can get any kind of greens in the market, but that's what I have a craving for. I can almost taste it on my tongue, smell its fresh green aroma.'

I saw a smile dart to her lips. 'Let me see what I can do,' she murmured.

The next morning Amma came in with a sheaf of leaves. I helped her strip the leaves off their branches, then left her to do her magic. I don't know what she did with a handful of dal, three red chillies and a colander of leaves. But I hadn't tasted anything like it before.

I called my mother to tell her about the wonder of the curry.

'I don't know what you're making such a fuss about. It must taste the same as the one I make,' my mother argued.

'No, it does not,' I retorted. 'There's no comparison.'

I ate the drumstick-leaf curry for lunch and dinner, with roti and rice. Savouring its viscosity, its aroma as it glided down my throat with every mouthful. Later that night, for the first time, I felt the baby move.

'Nonsense, it's much too early,' my husband mumbled, half asleep. 'You probably have indigestion. You shouldn't have crammed yourself silly today.'

I couldn't sleep. I lay on my back and watched the night ooze out through the window. For the first time since I knew I was pregnant, I felt afraid. A nameless dread about this life growing inside me. What if something was wrong with the baby? You heard stories all the time. Hole in the heart. Cerebral palsy. A cleft lip.

And I, what kind of a mother would I be? Did I have the patience, the understanding to be a good mother? I caressed my unborn baby, imagining its fine hair, the satin cheeks, trying to reassure the baby and myself in the process that everything would be all right.

In the morning I sat in the backyard, unable to shed the shadow of dread that had haunted me all night.

'Are you not well? Is something wrong?' I looked up to see Amma standing by my side.

'I thought I felt the baby move last night. And then I couldn't sleep. All night I kept thinking, will I be able to cope? This baby is going to change my life. How am I going to manage?'

There was understanding in her eyes. And a strange sadness. She took my hands between her palms and began gently rubbing them. 'You will cope. Don't worry about that. Women are made that way. Let me tell you a story...

'Once, long ago, there lived a woman. She had a husband who called her his queen, gave her all the comforts and filled her womb with three beautiful children. Every day the woman thanked the gods for the abundance of happiness she had been blessed with. One day the woman met a friend in the market who said, "I hate to tell you this, but I saw your husband in Mysore with another woman."

'A few days later, she found a letter in her husband's pocket. A letter from a woman in Mysore.

'Once, long ago, when the woman was a little girl, she shared a plate of food with another girl. When the woman's grandmother found out, she took a live coal from the fire and placed it on her tongue.

'"Never ever eat anyone's leftovers, do you understand?" her grandmother had said, applying a poultice to the spot where the coal had eaten into the flesh.

'The woman tried to ignore the letter, tried to still the memory of that day, but it was the little girl with the burnt tongue who said, "Please leave. I can't be your wife any more. Go back to the woman. Make her your queen, your wife, your whore, whatever. I don't want to see you, talk to you or even breathe the same air as you do for the rest of my life."

'The woman had three children, one just a baby. The woman didn't beg or sell herself. She took care of her children, their needs. Each time she went hungry, she said to herself, at least I've kept my self-respect through all this. She sent her children to good schools, helped them settle down, found them good life partners... all with the money she made from cooking idlis for a few small canteens.

'When I think of those days today, I wonder how I managed, how I coped. But God makes us women with a special ingredient. One little element that makes us go on, no matter how bad the odds are.'

This was my Amma. Short and plump, with a long braid that followed the steel of her spine. Slightly greying, meticulously clean, deeply religious, and highly fatalistic.

Please God, I prayed, make me just a little like Amma. Give me just an ounce of her strength, an inch of her determination to not buckle.

And then the baby moved again. 'Amma,' my voice rose in excitement, 'it moved again. Here, feel it.'

I placed her hand on my belly. Her face was ridged in concentration. 'I think I can feel it too,' she said softly, her voice tinged with awe.

We looked at each other and in the wonder of the moment I uttered the one single thought that had been hovering in my mind like a restless bee: 'I wish you were my mother.'

A picture of my real mother's face swam into the air between us, and for a moment we stared aghast at each other. Those were the words of a traitor. No matter how true they were, or how often you felt that way, to mouth them was a sin. Particularly when you had a living mother. I knew what was going on in her mind. How much she would resent it if someone came between her and her daughter. How much it would pain her if her daughter preferred someone else to her. I had made her feel like a trespasser infringing upon a relationship. The destroyer of a bond, unravelling the skeins that held it together. And nothing I said now would erase the feeling of guilt I had burdened her with.

Between us was the shadow of the unseen Roja.

I would have liked Roja to be an unfeeling monster woman. Callous of her mother's deep capacity for love, hurtful and negligent. It would have been so easy to plant myself in her place. Be the substitute daughter.

I watched Amma's eyes light up when she talked about her Roja. It was obvious that she preferred her daughter to her sons. 'Your sons are your sons only until they're married. Then they become other women's husbands,' Amma said as she bathed the baby.

She was sitting on a low-legged stool with her legs stretched out and her sari gathered around her knees. She laid the baby on her legs and gently bathed him. 'The other day we were watching something on TV and I saw a pair of earrings on a woman. So I told Roja, wouldn't something like that be nice? And do you know what my youngest son said? Yes, something like that would suit Selvi very well.' Selvi was the girl he was engaged to.

I sat beside her, content to hear her talk as she massaged oil into my son's skin. Moulding his brow, his nostrils, his lips into what she considered classical perfection.

She had taken charge of the baby the day I returned from my real mother's house. I had spent an uneasy time there, fraught with undercurrents and anxious moments. My mother couldn't decide who needed her more: a son with a torn ligament in his knee or a daughter with stitches in her shrunken belly. I had walked into a house that was hardly conducive to rejoicing. My father had sat across the table, tears in his eyes as he described the accident that would leave his son with a limp. The horror of imagining the death of a child, an adult son, had carved new lines in his face. I saw the glistening in his eyes, the anguish in his voice, yet all I wanted to do was scream. 'Don't do this to me. This is supposed to be the greatest experience of my life. I want laughter around me. I want to be surrounded by joy. Don't make me feel like my happiness has no place here!'

It is easy to believe that the birth of a new life reduces the intensity of sorrow that haunts a home. I thought that the gurgling sounds of a newborn would wipe the shadow from my father's eyes, stretch my mother's lips into a smile. I wanted to be the one to erase the pain in their lives. In return, I wanted to be petted, cosseted and allowed to lie dreamily with my baby by my side.

What I found was a set of parents wringing their hands in despair, impervious to the new baby, a brother angry with a destiny that had confined him to bed, and rooms echoing with unhappiness. When it was time to leave, I did so gladly. Maybe I paid to have Amma near me, but at least I knew that during the hours she was in my house, I mattered the most.

'The night before he was born, I dreamt of him,' she said,

slipping a gold ring onto his finger.

'I wished you were there when they wheeled me into the theatre,' I said.

'Did it hurt?' she asked anxiously.

'It doesn't any more,' I said, thinking how much at home the baby seemed, cradled in her arms.

She fed him, bathed him, played with him, indulged him. If it had been anyone else, I would have felt left out, even jealous of their special relationship. Somehow, with Amma I didn't feel threatened. She had her place. And I, mine.

Two months later, what had seemed marvellous became routine. The clock ticked and the light changed. Nothing else did. My eyes scanned a page without absorbing a word. My ears listened to the music but I may as well have been deaf. Nothing interested me. Not even the baby.

I watched the baby crawl all over the living-room floor. He tore a leaf off my precious philodendron, and I felt a cloud of rage swamp me. 'Let go, you brat,' I yelled, pulling him away from the plant and slapping his wrist. He looked bewildered at this frothing, fuming, shrew mother I had turned into. Then two giant drops trickled down his cheeks and his face crumpled into a wail.

Amma gathered him to her bosom and murmured, 'Hush, hush, my pet. Don't you realize your mother has had these plants longer than she's had you?' She gave me a strange look, but I turned my head away. I was ashamed of what I had done, but I wasn't going to admit it.

When the baby was asleep, she came to the backyard where I sat doodling, trying to escape the maze of manic moods I was trapped in. 'Why are you angry all the time?' she asked.

I tried to read her eyes. For censure, or disapproval. There was nothing there but kindness. Right then, that's what I wanted. Someone who would see my point of view and not dismiss it as post-natal blues.

So I told her. Of the emptiness I felt within me. A sombreness of spirit, a loneliness no one or nothing could alleviate; I felt that even my body had forsaken me. I told her of the marks that stretched across my belly, of the disgust I thought my husband must feel, each time he felt duty-bound to make love to me. All I wanted to do was curl into a heap in a corner and stay there for the rest of my life. I hated myself for turning into this pathetic mass of neuroses…

When I finished, she went into the kitchen and came back with a cup of tea. 'Drink this up,' she ordered. 'I think you should start looking for a job. You need to go out and start doing things once again. You need to stop feeling worthless. Don't worry about the baby. I'll take care of him.'

Once, long ago, I saw Amma mesmerized by a magazine cover. She stood in the backyard, all her chores forgotten, staring at it wistfully. I peeped over her shoulder to see what was so appealing about the picture. It was the side of a house with a door painted green and a path paved with round stepping stones and fringed with yellow primroses. Part of a tree was visible in the foreground, and there the picture ended.

So when we began building our house, I planned a room for Amma. It had a door painted green that opened into the garden. There was a path paved with stepping stones and borders in which yellow lantana would bloom. When it was built and ready, I invited her to move into the room, become a part of my life.

'No,' she said, 'I don't think so. Thank you for offering me this beautiful place. But I don't want to move. I'm content where I am.'

Two weeks ago, Amma opened the gate and walked in. When she clicked the latch shut behind her, it reverberated forever. She carried a suitcase and the branch of a tree.

'If you still want me to come and live here, I would like to,' she said quietly, as though mouthing the words cost her a great deal of effort.

She planted the branch in a corner of the garden and settled into the room. I waited for her to tell me what had triggered the change of mind. She would, I knew, in her own time.

And now, as we stood looking at the crown of leaves on the branch she had planted, it seemed as if that moment had arrived.

'When they sold the lease of the tenement I stayed in, I wasn't too perturbed. Then they brought the bulldozers in to demolish the houses and I still wasn't upset. After all, they'd found us another house to stay in, quite close by. Everyone made a hue and cry, saying how can you ask us to abandon our home of several years? And I said, what's the fuss, it's just bricks and mortar.

'Then they decided to cut the tree and I couldn't bear to live there any more. How could I? The tree had been part of my life for so many years. When I asked my husband to leave, no one saw me cry or heard my pain except the tree. I know you think of me as a strong woman. I saw you compare your mother to me and ask yourself why she couldn't be as tough, as capable and as impregnable to the world. But I was all that only because of the tree. The drumstick tree.

'Do you know the story of King Vikramaditya and the vampire that lived in the branches of a drumstick tree? Of how it helped him fathom the meaning of life?

'This tree housed all the vampires of my past. Each time I felt I couldn't cope, I sought refuge at its foot. And it would allow me to unburden myself of the blood-sucking, demoniac nature of my woes. In its branches I hung all the vampires of my life. And the tree accepted them all without protest.

'I could tell it what I could tell no one else. It was the repository of my confidences, the treasury of my hopes and the vault of my memories. Do you know what I called it? Amma. The tree was my friend, my companion, my provider. Every evening I prayed to it, asking for the strength to go on. "Help me, Mother," I would say. And in a dream, the mother spirit of the tree would appear and tell me what I ought to do next.

'And so, when they swung an axe through its heart, I felt the blow on my chest. And as the bark tore, I felt my flesh shred. I saw the tree bleed, heard its roots cry out as the branches keeled and fell over and its spirit wail as it was set adrift. And for the first time, I felt alone and afraid and old. As if I had no one...'

I didn't know what to say. A parrot disentangled itself from the green of the leaves of a mango tree nearby and rose into the sky, its wings fluttering, its screech raking the air.

Maybe she would always see me as a usurper trying to take her daughter's place. Maybe she would never care for me the way she did about her tree. But she was here. And would be for the rest of her life. That was all that mattered.

the hippoman

It hangs there in the cupboard. Breathing in through its many pores the combined fragrance of mothballs and air-freshener, and the mustiness of damp. A muddy grey, it falls from the outstretched arms of the hanger, the skin of a beast from which the soul has fled. Limp, lifeless and deceptively calm.

Do not be fooled. Within it lurks a monster. You can't touch it, or feel it. But if you were to zip yourself into its hide, it would grab you by the throat. Pierce your flesh with its claws, knot your tendons into a ball of twine and suck you dry of your soul.

The beast hasn't got a heart you can appeal to. Look into its eyes, forever focused on a point above your head. It stares with a blankness that defies emotion. Enormous lips line the cavernous mouth, which is pursed, entombing silence in its dark confines.

This is the beast that rules my life. Every day, I give myself to it, to do with as it pleases. To dominate and govern. In return, it gives me the keys to a kingdom. I am the king of a land populated by small furry creatures of the imagination. There are moments when I revel in my kingship of this nursery land. There are moments when the mantle of the beast overshadows me, so that I don't know any more whether I am man or beast.

It is these moments that take over my thoughts when sleep eludes me with the cunningness of a fox familiar with its territory. I think I may never have found expression for this spectacular being that exists in technicolour, in the depths of my mind. That I may have lived life without ever knowing what I'm capable of. That I may have remained what I am without the hippo-suit: an insignificant man with an insignificant destiny.

I think of what I would have been if Lewis hadn't relinquished the hippo-suit to me. So, it is with Lewis my story ought to start...

There never was a store like this. Its façade stretched a thousand feet long. Each one of its windows was the size of a little room inhabited by families of mannequins, each group portraying a slice of life. A birthday party, a great time at the beach, a day at the zoo... You could stand there all day, peering, nose pressed to the giant plate-glass, while your mind went on daytrips to the lands the mannequins lived in.

Walk down the steps, and the magic still persists. A toy train runs around the parking lot, an open carriage drawn by ponies with pink plumes on their heads, which you can hop into for a ride. There is even a camel man. Then there is as much popcorn as you can eat, huge dollops of ice cream in cones, sticks of cotton candy and heart-shaped balloons you can send into the clouds when you tire of holding them. All you have to do is walk into the store.

The day they opened the store, the traffic stood still at the junction. Lights changed, horns hooted and tooted, voices rose, fists waved. And then, mysteriously, the men and their machines were bewitched by the fantasy unfolding before their eyes. 'I know that creature,' a voice whispered. 'That's Humpty Dumpty.'

Lord, oh lord, this is childhood revisited. They were all there. Our friends from nursery land, whom we had parted from so ungraciously. The Three Blind Mice. Little Miss Muffet. Old McDonald and all the farm animals. Bo-Peep and Old King Cole. And there was a grey lumbering hippo. 'What is that animal doing there?' someone hissed.

The huge, ugly, clumsy grey hippo opened its pink mouth wide, stuck its furry-felt, strawberry-red tongue out, turned its back and waggled its enormous bottom before breaking into a little jig.

Then the hippo sat itself on a little jaunty stool, took a guitar and struck a few chords. The crowd hushed in expectation. Once again, the nursery-land folk were sent into exile in favour of more adult amusement. Here was a rarity. Here was the star of the store. The singing hippo.

Once upon a time, the Hippoman had a dream. To create music the world would cherish as a precious pearl. Once upon a time, the Hippoman had a voice that soared into the skies. Once upon a time, the Hippoman had a name: Lewis.

The hotel-bookings he took on were just to keep the money coming in, he told himself. When he had saved enough, he would hire a studio, get the best sound engineer and launch himself. Meanwhile, he hoped somebody from the music industry would walk into the restaurant one day and discover him. Ten years ago, all of it had seemed possible.

And then, one day, a man in a pink suit walked in. All through the evening, he eyed Lewis. He saw the dexterity of the fingers that plucked at the strings. He heard the voice that soared above the incessant croaking of the bull frogs from the pool around the restaurant, and strove to rise beyond its tiled ceiling. He sensed the ambition, the dejection. All evening he sat there, the man in the pink suit, sipping a fruit drink and toying with his glass noodles and mixed vegetable salad. When Lewis finished for the day, the man in the pink suit slipped a hundred-rupee note into Lewis' hand, gave him a card and asked him to give him a call.

Lewis turned over the card once, twice, a dozen times before he made up his mind. He put it into his wallet, got into bed and drew the quilt to his chin. He curled his toes and stretched them as his mind pondered the significance of the card. Something told him it was no ordinary happening. His life and his luck were going to change.

Lewis stumbled through a maze of beams and unplastered walls. This was where the voice on the phone had said they could meet. Amidst the dust and workmen, Lewis found him. In a mauve suit and a psychedelic tie that could hypnotize you if you stared at it too long. The man had a name. Reddy. And a proposition. A store, like the city had never seen before.

'But where do I fit in?' Lewis asked, bewildered. 'I'm not a salesman.'

'I don't expect you to stand behind a counter and do any selling. I don't even expect you to know what merchandise is in stock and what isn't. I want you to sing and manage a musical troupe,' Reddy coaxed. 'You will have all the freedom you want. You can sing what you please. We'll even cut a disc of your songs and market it. All I insist on is, you let me decide what your costume will be.'

That was how Lewis became king of the nursery land, in the foyer of the world's cutest store for kids. He was given a month's time to put his troupe together. 'They'll have to pitch in and sell in the store every once in a while though,' Reddy had warned him, when Lewis led us all into the store to meet him. None of us had a proper job or any hope of finding one. And we had one other thing in common: our love for music.

To us it seemed that Lewis was our messiah, leading us to a job that would answer the need in us to make music.

We were willing to do anything for him. Work long hours, stand behind counters and wear grins and even sweep the floors if necessary. And then we saw the costumes we were meant to wear.

'But Lewis, how can we…?' Something in me cringed at the thought of having to cavort in such a ridiculous costume in front of the whole world.

Lewis had smiled, his long lean face creasing into crinkles of amusement. 'Do you see this?' He gestured to a muddy-grey costume. 'This is what I will be wearing. The silliest costume of all. At least you guys will look cute.'

Lewis began zipping himself into the costume as he talked. We stared, unable to believe what we were seeing.

'Go on, tell me how I look,' Lewis said, striking a silly pose.

We giggled. We smirked. We laughed till tears rolled down our cheeks and ran into our mouths. We had never seen anything as silly as this. I thought I would pop an artery laughing, till Lewis discovered the cunning little opening through which he could move his hands freely, and the little slit that allowed him to breathe and sing.

Lewis picked up his guitar, struck a chord and began to sing. Lewis's voice was proud and strong, pure and clear, incongruous with the ugly body that clothed it. We watched him in amazement and awe. We saw in him the makings of a legend. And Reddy knew his hunch had been right.

Lewis liked being a star. He loved the way children clamoured for a place by his side. He liked, even better, the spell he cast on the women with his music. He basked in the envious glances the men threw at him as they wondered what it was about the ugly grey hippo that exuded such charisma.

Life had never been more delightful. All day he sang what he pleased. Ballads. Old Jazz tunes. Blues and Soul and Country. And never did he sing a request. Once, on a whim, he rewrote the words of an old Sammy Davis Jr. song and that became an anthem.

Children tumbled all around him, begging him to sing 'The Hippoman Song'. Inside the hippo-suit, Lewis grinned. If only they knew, he thought as he strummed the guitar and began to sing:

'The Hippoman!

Oh, the Hippoman came with his pretty songs...'

The Hippoman made good newspaper copy. The city magazine did a four-page feature with big glossy photographs, and some newspapers mentioned him as the new wave-maker in town. He was the mascot that mounted billboards and adorned signages. His face beamed from T-shirts and coffee mugs. He signed autographs with a flourish and every once in a while, obliged a parent by allowing a child to perch on his lap for a photograph.

As the legend of the Hippoman gained popularity, his powers too spread beyond the nursery land. Reddy liked him to sit in on every meeting. Promotions, festive discounts, bargain sales, even window-dressing ideas—the Hippoman had an opinion on everything. When a floor manager had a problem, he approached the Hippoman first. It was well known throughout the store that if you had the Hippoman's support, Reddy was at least willing to listen, instead of biting your head off the moment you opened your mouth.

Lewis loved all the attention he got. He walked with a swagger, and could hardly be bothered to give us the time of day. It hurt us alright. He was the friend we had all made music with. He was the guy who was game for a mug of beer any time. He was a good, fun person and suddenly Lewis had turned into the management, looking at the big clock pointedly if any of us took a few minutes extra during the breaks.

But none of us, including me, Lewis's oldest friend, dared say anything to him. For, after all, a few weeks ago, at a staff party, when someone was mimicking how Lewis played the Hippoman, Reddy had said, 'If I were you, I'd be careful what I said about Hippoman. When I move on to bigger things, he's going to be your boss.' And he'd laughed loudly and wagged a finger at the Hippoman.

Surely that laugh meant it was in jest. But no one was willing to take a chance. Not even I.

Popo the Clown spoke with a French accent. He was half French and half Indian, but said that he didn't know whether he was in spirit a Frenchman or an Indian. He was, he said, still seeking an identity.

He was plump, with round cheeks and chubby arms. His smile stretched from ear to ear and his eyes glittered with the merriment of baubles on a Christmas tree. He joked, he mimed, he sang and he juggled. He made you laugh till your sides ached, tears rolled down your cheeks, and all you wanted was to get your breath back. Sometimes, when Popo could be persuaded to, he read palms. And then he became a different man. He was all concentration and seriousness. But the moment he finished, he would switch off and become the grinning clown again.

It was just before the holiday season that Reddy began talking of variety. 'The nursery land is fine, but we need something more. Something that's new. What do you think, Lewis?'

The Hippoman nodded and chewed on a toothpick. The past year had been the best in forty years of living. The contentment had grown and spread, padding his waist and haunches, his neck and jowls. Oh yes, our Lewis was beginning to resemble the creature that he lived within most of the day.

'How about a clown?' he suggested. Lewis was being very careful. He didn't want a musician who might usurp his place. A clown he was sure would pall after some time. After all, how many jokes can a man make?

Reddy stared hard at Lewis and then clapped him on his shoulder. 'Perfect! I knew I could trust you to come up with a brilliant suggestion. A clown it shall be.'

Rumour had it that for that suggestion, Lewis received a hefty incentive in a white envelope. The stars, it seemed, were rallying again for the Hippoman.

But stars are fickle patrons. From their lofty heights, they chance on a destiny and let their stardust settle on it. Often, for no reason except the sheer boredom of doing the same thing day after day, they tire of illuminating a destiny and switch off. And then they scour the earth for a new victim. Astrologers refer to this as the passing of a phase. The waxing and waning of fortune. Just when you have beguiled yourself into a false sense of security, the stars do something to disturb it. The stars love upsetting apple carts, houses of cards, and lives. They detest complacency. And so they seek you out if you show signs of being happy in your skin.

Poor Lewis. He had it coming. He wore his contentment easily. All the world was a hippo-suit in which he dwelled comfortably.

Popo, we thought, would leave after some time. But, contrary to expectations, Popo was a hit and Lewis grudged him his popularity. Lewis was rude to him and openly hostile. He would cut in when Popo was juggling with oranges and lumber off with an orange, breaking Popo's momentum. And how the children laughed when they saw the Hippoman wag his bottom at the clown and stick his tongue out. Behind his greasy skin, Popo's mouth would droop and his eyes would cloud over. We were all sorry for him, but we didn't dare cross Lewis by showing our sympathy.

Lewis did everything to ruin Popo's act. But he had overlooked the one other talent Popo had. Reddy was a superstitious man and was forever referring to the almanacs and meeting soothsayers. Popo was just biding his time till he managed to get Reddy to himself for a moment. The next thing we knew, Popo had disappeared into Reddy's room and stayed there for several hours. When he came out, he wore a strange expression. That evening the stars decided to abandon Lewis.

'It's all his doing,' Lewis mumbled from across the table.

'What?' I asked in surprise, trying to gulp down the hot tea as fast as I could without scalding my tongue. Ten minutes was all we had to drink a cup of tea, smoke a cigarette and use the loo.

'He's been reading Reddy's palm and now the fool can't stop talking about him. Reddy says that as the mascot of the company, I ought to be moved away from the entrance. He's been doing some mumbo-jumbo charts for Reddy, and now he wants me to wait here till they decide on a new position for me. That pipsqueak doesn't know who he's messing with. He'll find out soon.' Lewis glowered at the teacup as if it was Popo with a handle.

I slipped back to nursery land and spread my tidbit of news. The truth is, all of us were a little tired of Lewis's tyranny. He no longer treated us as friends. Lewis was king and he made us aware of the chasm between him and us, with every word and gesture he used.

'Good for Popo,' Bo-Peep muttered.

'What do you think he'll do, though?' Humpty Dumpty asked.

'Knowing Lewis as we all do, you can be sure he'll make Popo's life miserable,' Old King Cole said under his breath, loosening his brocade dressing gown and blowing some air down his chest. It was one of those clear days when the sun shone relentlessly, drying the moisture off leaves.

'Hush,' whispered one of the Blind Mice. 'She is coming this way.'

Little Miss Muffet swayed towards us. Lewis and she had an arrangement. Some nights she stayed over at his place. Here in nursery land she seldom left his side. Once in a while they even sang duets together. It meant just one thing. He did care for her. Or he would never have let her share even a crumb of his glory.

'Hi guys,' she breezed as she drew closer. 'Have you seen Lewis?'

Then she stopped in mid-stride and her mouth fell open in shock. We turned to look at what was causing the horror on her face. The Hippoman stood in a corner of the entrance veranda, almost obscured by the giant waffle cone and chocolate-chip ice-cream cut-out. He stood there, forlorn jaws gaping, tongue hanging out, clutching his guitar.

'Oh, my God!' Little Miss Muffet said again and again. 'He must be boiling in that suit. There isn't an inch of shade there. Why is he standing there?'

We looked aghast at each other. This was worse than we had expected. And it dawned on us that Popo was no simple clown, content to laugh and be laughed at. Popo intended to get even, one way or the other.

For a week the Hippoman endured the ignominy. Lewis suffered when families walked past him, barely registering his presence. Lewis grit his teeth and clenched his fists when he saw Popo usurp his place. For a week his pride saw him through.

During the break, the Hippoman would sit silently, drinking his tea and chewing on a matchstick till it became a soggy pulp. He barely glanced our way and mostly ignored even Little Miss Muffet. It was like Lewis blamed us all for what was happening to him. How would all this end, I wondered.

Then one day Popo was eating his lunch, taking tiny bites out of a sandwich to protect his greased-on grin, when Lewis walked up to him. He thrust his palm out and growled, 'I hear you read palms. Do mine, will you?'

Popo continued to chew as he stared into Lewis's eyes unflinchingly. Then he said, 'Have you heard of the word please?'

The rest of us gasped. But Lewis didn't say anything. Instead, he stood there chewing on yet another matchstick as if he were trying to make up his mind. A long moment later, he said grudgingly, 'Please. Will you please look at my palm?'

Popo's greased-on grin came alive. He dusted his hands and said, 'Sure.'

We heaved a sigh of relief. Maybe things would work out between them. Maybe life would go back to being the way it used to be.

The clown peered at the Hippoman's palm. He traced a line with his forefinger and felt the ball of his thumb. He mumbled to himself and pressed his knuckles to his temples.

'Do you want to hear the truth or do you want to hear what you would like to hear?' Popo asked.

Lewis sucked in his breath. 'The truth.'

'Well, first of all, you have a very unusual hand.'

Lewis gleamed at that. Lewis always fancied himself to be special.

'There is fame in your destiny. Fame and prosperity. You will never feel the lack of anything material in your life. Not that it was always like this. There was a period when you touched rock bottom. See this configuration here. It means trials. Am I right? Is that how your earlier life was?'

Lewis's face was a study in amazement. This stranger was laying bare his life. He leaned forward eagerly, his voice syrupy with the willingness to please. 'I don't know how you do it, but everything you've said is the whole unadulterated truth.'

Strangely, I felt a deep sense of unease. Popo had never read my palm nor had I ever seen him do it before. He was just making educated guesses, manipulating the person in front of him and taking advantage of the chaos he was causing in the person's mind. Lewis was playing into his hands. No sooner had I thought this than I heard Lewis say, 'But that's all in the past. Tell me more. Tell me about my future.'

Popo cleared his throat. He stared at Lewis's palm. 'Your line of fortune is very strong. See this line. This is what you make of your life. And your hand is the hand of an achiever.

'Oh oh, but see this maze of lines here. It indicates a terrible period in your midlife. Disgrace and falling from favour. Humiliation and soreness of heart. And such mental anguish that you might even contemplate killing yourself.'

Lewis pulled his palm back. 'I don't believe you. You're just making it up.'

Popo got up and spoke to the room in general. 'This is the problem. People don't like hearing the truth. I did ask you, and now you don't believe me. That's your problem. Ask any one of them and they'll tell you how accurate my readings are.'

'I don't need to,' Lewis retorted. 'Maybe you told them the truth. But this,' he continued with a flourish of his hands, 'you are making up.'

Popo shrugged. 'Fine. If that's what you want to think. All I did was tell you what destiny has in store for you.'

Lewis's eyes blazed. 'You are the one who is playing with my life. Not destiny. You son of a bitch, do you think I don't realize what you are up to?' Lewis said quietly.

There was silence in the room after Lewis walked out. There was a certain stature in the way he carried himself. A pulling in of the stomach, a pushing out of the chest, an erectness to the back, as if he were preparing himself to battle for his dignity.

Popo looked around the room, trying to gauge our expressions. Then he broke into a laugh, as if to inject into the room that old feeling of camaraderie he shed around him. Only this time his laughter carried a trill of malice, an affectation of falseness. 'What's wrong with him?' he said to no one in particular.

None of us spoke a word. None of us liked him very much at that moment.

Lewis went to see Reddy. He stood waiting outside and I kept him company. There was no longer any question of divided loyalties. I wanted Lewis to know that he could count on me for anything. Lewis smiled at me. 'Strangely, this reminds me of the first time I went to meet him.'

Reddy was busy as usual. Where once he would have fitted in the Hippoman without a second thought, time was at a premium today.

'So how have you been, Lewis?' Reddy asked, shuffling a few papers on his desk.

'Not so good, sir,' Lewis said quietly.

Reddy looked up in surprise. He had expected trouble, but not open rebellion. 'And why is that?' he said with a frown.

For the first time, Lewis took a good look at Reddy. His garish suit and chunky jewellery. The cologne he wore like a neon sign and his smile that was too white to be true. And he made up his mind that this man would not be allowed to govern his life.

'It is this new position you have given me, sir,' Lewis began.

'What about it?'

'Firstly, no one comes that side. Which means I don't get to entertain as much as I used to. And sir, it is much too hot to stand there all day in a hippo-suit.'

'Is that all? I'll take care of that. I'll get someone to fix a beach umbrella there.'

'But what about my singing?' Lewis's voice rose in vexation.

'I don't know what you think, but let me tell you that my customers come here to shop, not to hear you sing. Let's get one thing straight, Lewis. You are just an accessory to the shop. A kind of a living, talking, singing commercial and nothing more,' Reddy said harshly.

'It is in my best interest and the shop's best interest that I allotted that place to you. Take it or leave it. I can always find another out-of-work musician to fill a hippo-suit and strum a few chords.' Reddy bent to look at the open file in front of him and said dismissively, 'You will have to excuse me now, I'm busy.'

Little Miss Muffet dunked a biscuit in her tea and sucked it into her mouth. Thoughtfully, she said to me, as I sat trying to improvise my blind mouse act, 'Lewis ought to be an unhappy man. But he's not. That's what worries me. Do you think it has affected him up here?' She pointed to her temple.

'What do you mean?' I asked.

'Well, he's working out. He's cut his hair in a new style, and I see him practice juggling, and once I caught him making faces in the mirror. And the other night he asked me for my lipstick and he drew a huge pair of lips around his mouth and spoke to me in a different voice... so unlike his rich, deep tones. He went like this...' she said, mimicking a clear, light, gay voice. A clown's voice.

I was stumped. What was Lewis planning to do? Make a comeback as a clown?

It was a Friday evening, one of our busiest times, when Lewis grabbed the horns of his recalcitrant destiny and brought it to its feet.

The Hippoman stood strumming his guitar moodily. Nobody paid him any attention. Everybody hovered in the section where Popo was. The children watched as he walked on stilts and juggled cups with great dexterity. The children clapped and clapped when Popo finished his act. 'Hang on there, kids,' he cried, 'help your Mummy choose what you want to buy, and meanwhile I'll be back before you can say Popo the Clown.'

When he came back, Little Miss Muffet was sitting on a fibreglass rock, spooning curds into her pouting mouth. He went to stand behind her and made faces that made even the grown-ups grin. Then the clown fell on his fours, splayed his arms and feet and crept up to Miss Muffet, pretending to be a spider. Little Miss Muffet squealed in fright like she was meant to. But the spider didn't go away.

He just crept closer and closer until he'd pushed her back onto the rock crop. Little Miss Muffet's screams now filled the store. When the tongue of the spider clown darted into Little Miss Muffet's mouth, she ceased screaming to exclaim in surprise. But the tongue allowed her to say no more and slid deeper into her mouth, devouring, silencing. And as if to match the tongue's bold forays, the clown's hand crept under her skirt.

The children stared. Mothers and fathers stared. For a moment, even the mannequins craned their necks and stared. Then the spell broke as Little Miss Muffet began to scream again. Voices rose. When Reddy came to discover the cause of the commotion, he heard several garbled versions.

'But where the hell is he?' he asked, his mouth tightening.

Someone murmured, 'He walked off as if he'd done nothing wrong. I think he went down the stairs.'

When Reddy walked into the staffroom, Popo the Clown was sipping a cup of tea. Reddy stood in the doorway staring at Popo. When he spoke, his voice had a molten-steel casing to it. 'You have exactly two minutes to clear out of here. Your settlements will be made by cheque and mailed to you. Now get the hell out of here.'

Popo stared, bewildered, horrified. 'But why?'

'Why?' Reddy spluttered. 'They were right. You are cool. If you wanted to kiss Miss Muffet, you should have done so on your time. How dare you risk the reputation of my store?'

'Kiss Miss Muffet?' the clown repeated. 'Why should I? I don't know what you are talking about.'

'Get out!' Reddy bellowed. 'I don't want to hear any more concoctions.'

Reddy walked to his room thoughtfully. It wasn't going to be easy wiping that ugly scene off people's minds. But first he would have to make peace with Lewis. Only the magic of the Hippoman could save the store's image.

The Hippoman zipped his suit on for the last time. It had served its purpose, but it was time to move on.

'What can I say that will make you change your mind?' Reddy pleaded.

'Nothing,' Lewis said gently. 'You said take it or leave it. I am leaving it. But I do have a suggestion to make, for whatever it's worth. He'll make a good Hippoman,' he said, pointing to me.

'After all, you just need a voice to fill a hippo-suit.' And

Lewis smiled and gave me a conspiratorial wink. It was his way of rewarding me for my part in his act of revenge. I had kept Popo talking in the staffroom while Lewis had turned into Popo the Clown for a few minutes.

Reddy looked stricken. Suddenly his whole world was falling apart.

'What are you going to do?' I asked Lewis.

'I am going to sing all my favourite songs now.'

'No, I mean like tomorrow, like in the future.'

Lewis took a deep breath. 'I'm going to take off. Go on a holiday, see a ruin by moonlight, paddle in the waves, ride a camel, do all those things I never had a chance to do before.'

'And then?' I probed, sure there was more.

'And then, I'm going to cut a disc. I'll be Lewis. Not a voice in a hippo-suit.'

I stare at the hippo-suit hanging in the cupboard lifelessly. And then, slowly, the thought of wearing it weighs down my shoulders. I have a kingdom to rule. Songs to sing. People to entertain. I don't feel any joy at the thought. I only feel trapped.

come to bed, my pretty

There he sits. Tie-and-dye-robed, apple seeds coiled around his neck, beaming an aura of flower power. There he sits, deep in thought amidst his pots, roots, tubes, herbs, and the black cat with the raspberry tongue.

There he sits, weighed down by the burden of a lineage of discoveries. A granduncle had caused veins of gold to varicose hillsides. Great granddad had turned princes into toads. As for his father, he had built palaces with a sweep of his hands.

There he sits by the hearth, scratching the black cat's neck and staring into the fire. All day and night, he broods on the thought that life is passing him by.

Then an impulse makes him leap from his rocking chair. Into a pot he throws a handful of ash, a measure of sand and a dozen sea shells. He places the pot on the fire to melt and bubble.

There he sits, keeping vigil over the fire that leaps up the chimney.

Now he rises and walks to his stewpot. He takes a reed and gently twirls it in the pot, collecting a gob of the molten mass. He puts the reed to his mouth and blows into it a strange melody that will coax the gob to take on a form.

All through the night he blows, and as the sun begins to colour the sky, he eases the form off the pipe and lays it among the glowing coals. He lies in his bed and watches. The break of day. The birth of glass.

Unknown to him, a little blob of glass flies out of the window. Dewdrop-like, it lodges in a heart. Bang the glass drop with a hammer; it won't break. Snip the curve of its tail and it will shatter.

Bella is not a queen. Bella is not an empress. Bella is not the fisherwoman who became an empress and then a fisherwoman once again.

Bella is a princess. Bella likes to sit in her tower and comb her hair. Bella likes to feel the teeth of the comb graze her scalp. Bella likes to hear her hair sing.

Bella is waiting. Bella waits for the hooves to drum beneath her tower. Bella waits to hear a white stallion neigh and snort. Bella waits for the knight on the white steed. Bella waits for the knight to rescue her from the dragon. Bella waits for him to prove the magnitude of his love for her. Bella waits with her heart hanging out.

The strands of Bella's hair are the strings of a harp. Shall we call them harpies then?

Part-woman, part-monstrous filament, every strand has a tale to tell. When the teeth of the comb pluck at them, they let loose little notes: Bella's dreams.

Do...you know she dreams he'll fight the fiercest demons for her? *Re*...member that she never pauses as she keeps winding us round her fingers. *Me*...Well, I think she will when she can snip a lock of us and give it to him to wear on his breast. *Fa*...ah! *So*...I didn't know! I know she thinks she'll inspire him to perform superhuman feats. *La*...rgely her fantasies revolve around how much he'll cherish her. *T*...ill he comes, she's prepared to wait.

Bella's mixed up her fairy tales. Bella is wide-eyed Goldilocks. Bella is the Ugly Duckling who became a swan. Bella is Sleeping Beauty and Rapunzel. Bella is the Snow Queen whose kiss is colder than glass.

Bella is like the glass drop in her heart. Within her is a state of permanent turmoil. And so I can blow, mould, spin or draw her into any shape, texture or mood. But I can never force her.

Maybe in glass Bella sees a kindred spirit. She has always been attracted to glass.

I've bought her glass. Several kinds. Stained glass, shimmering glass, opaque glass, etched glass, cut glass, whorls of glass, glass with lights teased into them.

But all those pieces of silica and sand never mattered. She just held them in her hand for a moment, pressed her lips to mine dutifully and left them on the nearest table. There they would lie, gathering dust and neglect. Until I put them away in the cabinet and displayed to myself how little I seemed to reach out to her.

Nothing but that glass would do. I watched how your eyes searched for it every time we visited the Fernandes home. I could see how much you coveted it. And I wondered why you found it so attractive.

What was it, after all? Just a souvenir from a bar in America. A goblet that served a cocktail and had the bar's name on it. A leftover from someone's holiday. And it was this meaningless piece of glass you'd lost your heart to.

Remember I did tell you I could arrange to get one such glass for you. Remember I even promised to take you there some day. But that wasn't what you wanted. It had to be the

Fernandes's glass and nothing else.

The glass. Suddenly it was a symbol. Something you flashed in my face to say, prove it, prove that I'm worthy of such love. Show me how much you love me, get it for me and show me how much.

Tonight I am the knight. I am the price. Tonight I am the creator of fairy-tale endings.

Look at me, Bella. I am not your handsome hero. My chest doesn't span the universe. I am just an average man with average powers.

You didn't think I would do it, did you? You didn't think I'd risk my reputation and everything else I'd worked so hard to acquire.

You sit there coiling a strand of hair around a finger. You sit there with a glassy indifference. You sit there as if there is nothing that I can say or do to wake you up. You sit there in the car. Waiting.

I stand in front of the five-foot high wall draped with a creeper. I press my gloved hands on its spike-driven top, and lever myself to rise.

There. I've scaled the wall. Three dogs roam the grounds. I wait for them to get my scent. The dogs know me and yet they growl. For them I have meat well-marinated in a mixture of cough syrup and powdered valium. Silly mutts, see how easily they let themselves be doped. One of them even licks my hand.

My rubber soles don't disturb the silence of the night. I walk across the lawn and towards the dining room. This is easy.

Satyr of the Subway

Earlier in the evening, when we were here for dinner, I had unlatched a window. I climb in through it now. I am inside and everything is familiar. I need to get my breath back. I walk into the living room and sit on an armchair. The glass is upstairs on an open shelf and between me and the glass are twenty-five steps. Each step for a year we've spent together.

Twenty-five years and there is still about you an air of waiting. A holding back. A remoteness. An aura of touch-me-not.

It isn't enough for you that I love every inch of you. Your now-not-so-firm breasts, the corners of your mouth that droop, the looseness of your abdomen, the blue veins, the crow's feet, the lines on your throat, your flaccid thighs...

It isn't enough, my love, is it? That I filled your womb with children and your breasts with milk? It isn't enough that I stayed awake at night to change the nappies and make the bottle. Or that I rocked the cradle while you slept with your hair draping the pristine pillowcase.

It isn't enough, my dear Bella, is it, that in all these years I have never lusted for another woman? It didn't mean a thing to you, did it, that every evening I rushed home to be with you? Or that I've never wanted to be anywhere but with you?

You sit there in the car, the engine switched off, your eyes closed. Your hair ripples. Such lovely hair. Such lovely eyes. But not for me. Are they, my lovely?

Twenty-five years of waking up first to make you a cup of tea so that you could begin your day bright-eyed. Twenty-five years of letting you read the newspaper first. Twenty-five years of watching your eyes glaze and look beyond me as I gathered you in my arms. Twenty-five years of believing you needed your orgasm before I did. Twenty-five years of consideration and affection.

It just isn't enough, is it?

I walk up the steps. Slowly. One at a time. No hurry.

I take the glass and drop it into the felt-lined bag I have with me. In its place, I leave a little glass frog. Maybe the Fernandes family will think a leprechaun visited them. Maybe they won't even notice it. As I walk out of the house, there is a strange singing in my veins.

For tonight I am the gallant who has tilted at more than windmills. Tonight I'll smash the glass you've locked yourself into. Tonight I'll draw a response from you, body and soul. Tonight, my princess, your time is up. Tonight, my love, we'll rumple the sheets with more than sleep.

a prayer for sax

The night is damp velvet, oozing blackness in giant drops.
A darkness that shadows everything that dares disturb its
fabric. A steady hum rises through the air. A glint of silver; a
flash of life. Who dares to be out on such a night when only
demons stir?

Heady with freedom, the demons leap into the air, whooping
and screaming, letting out the pent-up frustration of not being
allowed to walk the earth when they choose. Breath turns into
fog that curls and seeks a victim. Tonight is all they have, to do
as they please—evoke fear, take a life, spread sorrow...
Tomorrow they will have to be back in their loamy prison six
feet deep in the ground.

The hunt is on. And as the hum perforates the fog, they
scent blood. The hum turns into a whine. Help, I can't see. The
demons laugh, splicing the skies with sheer joy and spewing
droplets of saliva in a fine piercing rain. Run, run, little boy,
let's see how far you can go...

As if it knows it has awakened fierce forces it should have
left alone, the pale silvery creature tries to retreat. The radar
beeps: a landing place to escape the clutches of the giant hands
that seem to reach from the horizon.

The demons freeze, tall, mountainous and blue-ridged in
the path the silvery moth has chosen to fly. Swirling fog with

every monstrous breath, casting the night as their net.

The silvery moth circles, searches and then as if it knows there is no other way to go, it plummets straight down. To where the faithful servant of the demons, darkness, awaits.

Far away on a radar, a red dot blips and then disappears.

The astrologer's voice reverberates through the room, bounces off the ceiling and clings to the air. The lamp flickers uneasily. Shadows splatter the walls, smearing the photographs. I watch the grey settle on my son's face and feel a strange sense of disquiet. There is nothing to this, I tell myself, but a few educated guesses and an understanding of my vulnerability.

I know what people say. They look at this big house and whisper among themselves, 'How do they live there all by themselves, rattling like two peas in a pod?'

My friends walk through the rooms of this house that echoes with emptiness and pity me. They pretend to be interested in the photographs that are everywhere. I see that look come into their eyes. The look that says, poor thing, she's trying to erase her loneliness with pictures.

It is true, you know. I miss you, my son. Sometimes I miss you so much that I can almost feel you here beside me. Strange, I get this sensation that you are in the room with me now and you are crying, 'Don't let me go. Hold me tight.'

My precious child, how can I let go of you? Can't you see how I surround myself with memories of you?

See this? It is you when you were two years old. Was there ever a child like you? Crinkly hair, crinkly eyes, crinkly smile. Darting through the rooms like sunshine, your laughter crinkling like waves. I was an impatient mother, my parents said. Did you think so too? They were horrified when they saw the collar and the leash. Later on, when you grew up, it was a favourite topic of conversation at family reunions: how I kept you chained to the window when I was busy in the kitchen. They never knew the million fears that ravaged my mind when I left you alone even for a moment. This way, I knew you were safe. This way, I could hold you to me even when my hands were busy. In the night, I would caress your ankle, trying to brush away the feel of the leather collar. I would kiss your brow till you fell asleep. And suddenly I would feel bereft because I couldn't follow you there, where you had wandered away to.

Here you are six years old. We took this one to send to my sister. In the middle of the day, I made you wear your pyjamas, tousled your hair and asked you to get in between the sheets. When I came back with the camera, you had fallen asleep. So I let you lie there while I shot your picture. When you woke up, you screamed for me. 'Larling!'

Larling. I love that name. It is our special bond. All day, that day, I walked with a song in my heart. I wasn't plain old mummy. I was Larling.

I hate this one. I hated it when you suddenly seemed to need me less and less. Every time I look at it, I see you poised for flight. Your face ridged with concentration, your eyes searching the horizon. The rope of the swing is taut as it pulls away from the branch of the old mango tree. I would watch in trepidation as you pushed the swing higher and higher, and heard the ominous creak of the branch protesting as the rope bit into the bark. Then, when the swing could go no higher, you would twist it till it arched and curved into the side of the tree dense with pepper vines. The swing would slam into the undergrowth, shattering the stillness of the afternoon, while you leapt off screaming, 'Crash-landing!'

And the air would grow heavy with the aroma of crushed pepper leaves, and the birds would screech in terror and emerge from the branches like bats out of hell. Year after year, we returned to the old family home where the mango tree waited like a malevolent giant. Until the year my mother died and I had it chopped down.

You stand there with your father, already as tall as he is. Proud to be his son, beaming your love for him. I'm still Larling, the mother you would lift off the floor in a giant hug, but it is Daddy who has begun to shape your dreams for you.

Here is another one with Daddy. You gaze earnestly into his face, your hands cupping your chin. Daddy had been telling you the story of his life. Of how he chose to go sailing in the oldest and most battered of ships, simply because he was paid more to do so. Of how if he had been a coward, he would have got no closer to the fulfillment of his dream. And it scared me so to see the spark light up in your eyes. He made it seem so easy. If you dare, you can do it.

I wanted to gather you to my bosom that day and plead with you, 'Don't, my son.' But I bit back my words. You were no longer Larling's baby; you were already Daddy's little man.

Sax. Is that a name or a being? Sometimes I think of it as a creature that has crept into you and taken possession of your soul, making you discontented except when you soar in the skies. Your shoulders stretch wide, your eyebrows are fat caterpillars. In your school graduation photograph, you already seem a full-grown man. And yet, when you smile impishly and call me 'Larling', I see traces of the little boy you once were.

Sax. I learnt to call you by that name. You wanted me to. A new country deserves a new name, you said. Sax reminds me of Icarus, I said. Sprouting little wings on his shoulders even as he walked the earth, dreaming dreams no mortal should. But you laughed it off, saying Icarus was a stupid son of a bitch with wax wings, while you were smart enough to depend on only the best aluminium. I let myself be comforted by your strength.

In this picture, you look like a young eagle that has just

discovered it can conquer the skies if it chooses to. The first time I put it up, my friends pointed out the discrepancy: 'What is a postcard doing amidst a cluster of family photographs?' I smiled and showed them the speck of a car parked beneath a tree. We took that picture of your car the first time you took me flying. As I felt the ground dissolve beneath our feet, I shuddered and thought this must be what death is like. A churning of the stomach, a whistling of air through the ears, a kind of nothingness, and this is what you slipped into, day after day. Then I glimpsed the exhilaration radiating from you and felt a great sorrow descend upon me. Already our worlds were so far apart.

This smooth-talking stranger can't be you. This is that creature Sax. Greed and ambition: how can you distinguish one from the other? When you pointed out the huge park with a grey mansion set in it and said, 'One day I'll have a home like this', I smiled because my little boy was talking like a man. Then you said, 'I want to be one of the richest men in the world.' And I couldn't help gasping.

'Oh, I know what you are thinking!' you continued, 'we have enough money. But I want more. I want so much money that no one will ever dare say no to me. Someday I want to come back to India and make everyone who made my Daddy suffer, weep in anguish.'

I didn't speak. How could I? I didn't want to seem a coward. I was afraid of losing the respect you had for me. So I grunted and stared at the Virginia countryside.

I would point out this one of you seated in your car and remark jokingly, 'My son is like a snail. He carries his home on his back.'

The first time I saw your car crammed with your books, files, music, your good suit in a plastic wrap and cartons of god-knows-what, I cringed in disbelief. Then I raged at Daddy.

'How dare you push him so?' I screamed at him in my head.

There is a stranger in this picture. She has a cloud of auburn hair and a porcelain complexion. You called up one night to tell me you were in love. You wanted me to tell Daddy about it. 'Please, Larling,' you said. 'She is everything you wanted my bride to be.' As if saying that would buy instant acceptance from me. How do you know what I wanted for you?

'Just look at the picture I'm sending you. We look perfect together.' How can you be sure, I wanted to ask. Photographs have no dimensions; they are just surface gloss. Are you in love with her because she comes up to your ear and her smooth skin sets off your craggy features? But these are things you say eye-to-eye and not over a crackling telephone line. So I said quietly, 'Are you sure? I just want you to be happy.'

I still can't look at this one without tears welling in my eyes. I should have been there too. I had planned this day for so long. How I would welcome your bride to our home with a necklace, a family heirloom. How I would lay it around her neck, fix the difficult clasp and then turning her around, I would lift her chin and say, 'Now I have a daughter too.' But you chose to get married in a hurry. What were you afraid of? That we would object? That we would put emotional pressure on you? How little you know us, son!

She's wearing the red and black sweater I knitted for you. You stand there, the two of you, cheek-to-cheek, arms linked. You look happy. But is it the kind of happiness that endures? Does she cook fish the way you like it? Does she dust your back with talcum? Does she remind you to put moisturizer on the dry patches on your face? Does she wait up for you when you come home late? Does she hold you tight when you have a nightmare?

This is the one I delight in the most. The place you made for me in your home and your life. You are a smart one, aren't you? You knew how much I would resent your wife if I felt any less important. And so you took care of it with a bedroom suite, fitted carpets and matching linen. 'This is your room,' you said to me. 'I want you to know that you are welcome in my home anytime you choose to come. I'll always love you, Larling.'

That night, I lay on the bed you had bought for me and knew for certain that you had become a man and never again would I see my little boy.

See this vacant spot. This is for the picture of my first grandchild. When you called last night to tell me that you would soon be a father, I felt my heart leap. I was going to see you as you once used to be, twenty-eight years ago.

The astrologer's voice scythes into my thoughts. 'Look at the lamp,' he says. 'Is it cracked?'

'No, of course not,' I reply.

'Why is the oil dripping? You do know what that means, don't you? A soul is leaving a body. The flame is flickering; the breath is draining.'

'What are you saying?' I demand.

'I'm not saying anything. I just don't like the omens. Even the sky foretells tears. It is grey and overcast. There is thunder in the air. Why does it feel like it must six feet deep in the ground?'

'You are scaring me,' I murmur, a snake of dread uncoiling within me.

'I didn't mean to,' he says quietly, 'it is just that tonight is the eve of the darkest night in the year. It is the time when the unhappy spirits still seeking a resting place emerge. They are not happy souls. They are vicious creatures looking to torment and create pain, as if by doing so they will feel less alone in their anguish. They choose for their malicious pleasure lives that are in no way prepared to die. Men in their prime, pregnant women, gifted children...these are their prey. For they know that here are souls that are unwilling to leave their earthly bodies and hence would join them in their restless wanderings.

'There is no reason why you should be affected, except that tonight marks the passing of a phase in your horoscope.'

The astrologer packs his board and cowrie shells. As he gets up, I place a hundred-rupee note on the table.

'I can't accept this,' he says.

'Don't worry. You don't have to feel guilty. You are just doing your job. It is up to me to accept what the planets foretell. I don't have to... Anyway, my son just called to say his wife is pregnant. Maybe that's what the passing of a phase is all about.'

'I hope so. In fact, I'll come back to write the child's horoscope and you can pay me then.' He pauses uncertainly. 'Will you ask your husband and son to be careful?' His eyes are bleak. But I choose to ignore them.

I stand at the door and watch him walk to the gate. I must call my son right away and ask him to avoid flying for the next two or three weeks. And I'll make a few offerings at the local temple. Between God and me, we will watch out for him. Anyway, why am I assuming that he would be the one? It could be me. It could be Daddy.

Then the telephone begins to ring...

Report from *The Roanoke Herald*

Late last night, a single-seater courier plane crashed into the Catskill Mountains. There was no damage to the aircraft except for the right wing, which was ripped away from the body, following the impact. However, the pilot, Sax Sekharan, a young Indian, died in the crash. Authorities have ruled out instrument failure. A source said they are still investigating.

a thanksgiving tale

The Thanksgiving turkey lay on its back in the manner of all roast turkeys. A sumo wrestler pushed to the ground, rotund legs with enormous thighs staring helplessly at the heavens. The breast, plump and proud with many days of force-feeding, glistened. The neck that had cackled, gobbled and gurgled in a turkey-throat now lay in a black garbage bag somewhere. The skin that was left as a reminder of that throat was stretched, tucked and pinned. A flaccid cock in Y-fronts.

Bread had been crumbled. Butter melted. Onions braised. Mince added. Herbs sprinkled. Stuff the bird and pop him in.

When he's done, place him on a platter and raise the carver. As the blade meets flesh, voice your choice. White meat or dark? Breast or drumstick? With a little of that delicious stuffing, of course.

Isn't there something we've forgotten? The bird is, after all, a symbol. And symbols don't amount to much unless a little blood is spilt around them. So cranberries from a can are puréed into a sauce and poured into a glass dish, to drench the slabs of meat. Redness everywhere.

The king of the table is carved into many portions. 'Eat as much as you want, please do, or we'll be eating turkey till Labor Day.' The subjects lie in their individual dishes and tureens, awaiting attention. Virginia ham, nectar-glazed, fragrant, succulent and golden-hued; fork a morsel and taste ecstasy. Giddy-headed, black-eyed peas swimming in a pool of collard greens. Sweet potatoes which had finally found a place beside the sophisticate aubergine and the humble stewpot staple, the baby carrot. Their sweet dumpy forms awaited. None of that 'always a bridesmaid, never a bride' syndrome.

Hello, but what is this unfamiliar group that huddles between the carrot cake and the pumpkin pie?

Two deep pots and one little dish. Fluffy rice with the lustre of seed pearls, raisins glinting garnet-like. An aroma of curry moves in a cloud, smothering the offerings of the Pilgrim fathers. In their little puddle of chilli-vinegar, smooth onions wallow. Serene in their sourness, they will never be crunched, munched, swallowed, digested and transformed into nothingness.

The breast of the turkey heaves. A rumble. A slow mumble that spreads through the table, until even the sweet little things, the cake and pie hiss, 'Who is this lying on our table?'

Sarah did a despicable thing. She sat by her window that framed the frozen stillness of the Hudson River, and called Mike. Only the lonely would have done such a despicable thing on that last Wednesday night in November.

The telephone trilled in seven rooms, on five floors. Yvonne, watching TV in her kitchen, eyed the telephone warily as she crumbled cornbread for her stuffing.

Callers on Thanksgiving Eve had only one motive.

Mike paused in his second-floor dining room. He had been checking to see if the dumb waiter was working. He knew what Yvonne would be thinking as the phone rang within arm's reach.

Hello, he said.

Hello Mike, a voice quavered back. His heart sank. Sarah. Lonely Sarah. Old Sarah. Sarah who had once lived in the same apartment block. Sarah who hadn't learnt to let go. In this city of flux and motion, neighbours were not friends you U-hauled along for the rest of your life. This was Manhattan. Where lights changed, parking meters ticked and people escaped their past with a change of address.

Hello Mike, the voice sought again.

He forced festivity into his voice. Mouthed pleasantries. He heard her say in that trembling voice of hers, 'Oh, I don't have anything planned for tomorrow. Maybe I will fry a piece of chicken and there's some Jell-O from Sunday's for dessert.'

He thought of the abundance that would grace his table. He thought of the leftovers that would pile up in the refrigerator. He thought of the food that even the dogs would refuse to taste after a week. He thought of the waste of grace. And he heard himself say those words that Yvonne didn't want him to. He threw open his home and asked Sarah to share the abundance that his table was blessed with.

He knew Yvonne would think Sarah despicable. And he also knew why Sarah had done it.

Sometimes the heart leaps over the mind, scatters pride, and forces people to do strange things. Sometimes he allowed his mind to salute that vagrant heart.

Yvonne could read the note of his footsteps. The patter when he was alight with excitement. The harsh clump when he was angry. The quiet reticence when he was hurt. The stop and go when he was unsure...

One, two, three, she counted as he walked down the wooden staircase. He paused. She waited.

Sometimes she thought there was nothing she didn't know

about him. Twenty years ago she had taken him in hand. He had sideburns, flares in his trousers and a sad lack of syntax in his spoken English. He loved gadgets, flashy ties, plastics and TV soaps. She moulded his tastes, taught him to dress in designer suits and introduced articles into his language. She had fashioned him into the man he was today.

But there was something she had never intruded upon. His visits to India. Every three or four years, he went away and she never said, don't go. She wasn't afraid that he would disappear from her life. She knew that when he returned, it would be with renewed desire for her, for the promise their life together held. It was the power of the spell she had cast. A spell wrought out of freshly-squeezed orange juice, dollar bills and the master-key properties of the American passport.

She patted the bird dry with a paper towel. Her chubby hands worked automatically. He had taken to the American way like a natural. He liked his steaks rare, his potatoes hashed and ice in his wine. He insisted on a turkey for Thanksgiving, a tree for Christmas and a barbecue over Labor Day weekend.

She began trussing the turkey, placing the middle of the string below the breast at the neck-end. He watched her from the doorway of the kitchen he had DIY-ed in the course of a summer. He had stripped the linoleum and the ugly green paper the earlier residents, a lesbian couple, had hung in the hundred-year-old brownstone.

He watched her bring the ends of the string over the wings and then underneath the bird. This way and that, until the ends of the drumstick were tied together.

In its knots, he saw himself. Suddenly he felt a wave of empathy with the bird. He felt her brush butter all over him. He could sense the heat of the oven opening before him. He could smell his skin sizzling.

She waited for him to tell her who had called.

Every year for Thanksgiving dinner, they pored over their guest list. Names were deleted and added until it represented a perfect mix of voices, mannerisms and professions.

There was Yvonne's family. Trudie, her sister, who'd been working in a supermarket in Philadelphia for more than ten years. She baked cakes, fretted about her children and never could understand how Yvonne was so talented. There wasn't any evidence of talent in her own family.

Chet, big, fat, slobbering, white Chet. He was a Xerox salesman given to taking out his frustrations lying on top of Trudie. Out of this weird co-habitation and repeated fornication was born Junior. Addicted to *Baywatch*, Wrigleys and Dad's collection of *Playboy*, he sauntered through life on Nike Air. Just do it was what he did.

This then was Yvonne's family. They saw each other once a year. The rest of the time, life was too fast for them to catch up with each other. Sometimes the car radio, in the midst of playing the best mix of the sixties, seventies, eighties and nineties, turned into a preacher advocating family ties—*you got to make a choice, to give your heart and voice, we're all connected... New York Telephones.*

There were times when Yvonne took a hiatus from designing cotton jersey and knitwear for exclusive boutiques, and called Trudie. But mostly, she ran a hand over her creations and called a buyer in Texas.

But let's get back to the guests who wait to be introduced. They hold glasses of California white and crunch the little samosas that Mike had bought from the Indian store. Little pouches of spice, potatoes and peas which Mike had fried to a golden-brown and arranged on a bed of lettuce.

Oh, look who is here! Costa. Don't you remember him from last year? Mike's friend from India. He paints, you know.

Costa, straggly silver hair and scruffy clothes, wore a

bemused smile. Alimonies and child support had eaten away his earnings. He lived in a rent-controlled apartment and continued to paint his tortured divinities. With him is Nisha. By day she went from art dealer to art dealer, peddling his paintings. At night she snaked her tongue around his tired scrotum, raked her fingers through his silver mane and tried to revive the dwindling soul in his art. Just so, later on, there would be no legacy problems (Costa was, after all, seventy-three years old), she fucked his son too. Breasts swinging, screeching like a bird of prey, she rode him, sucking his power, seeking to control.

Watch Nisha, will you? See how she eyes Gowri. Poor homesick Gowri, with her stick-on bindi and printed silk sarees. Gowri yearned for mangoes and hot summer afternoons. On her way home from the La Guardia hospital, where she was a doctor, she often bought a tin of jackfruit and cooked it the way her mother would have. With coconut and ground cumin; with red chillies and mustard seeds sautéed. But it never tasted the same.

Not that it mattered to Divakaran, her husband. He's done all kinds of things to make a living. He couldn't have done that in India. Between him and Mike was a bond of secrets. No one was telling on the other. Just as long as the occasional photographs of new cars, Central Park in summer and the Manhattan skyline found their way to their homes in India, nobody would suspect a thing.

Yvonne was very careful. She made sure that Mike's Indian friends could visit them. No point in creating a vacuum in his life. A vacuum that could have unpleasant repercussions.

She had her own guests, too. Stephen, half-Thai, half-German, a diva of the antique world. Roland, a black activist. And Kathy, who worked with CBS.

It was this room, where every guest was handpicked for a

reason, that Sarah walked into. A jarring note in that softly-lit room, fragrant with pot-pourri, cut flowers and tall candles made of real beeswax.

Sarah gushed. Sarah talked too much. Sarah flung her arms and gestured wildly. Sarah giggled. Sarah fluttered her eyelashes. Sarah, in those few minutes of walking into the room, dropped her purse, her glasses and then her stockings.

Yvonne looked at the pool of nylon around Sarah's scrawny ankles and felt embarrassed. For herself, her guests, for the woman at the mercy of a snapped suspender. All the good feeling that glass after glass of Moet had wrapped her in began to evaporate, to be replaced by an anger that was biting in its venom.

And so, even as she went to help Sarah, she remembered the despicable thing Sarah had done.

Many minutes later, wearing new flesh-tinted pantyhose, Sarah sat in a chair with a smile screwed onto her face. She turned her head this way and that, taking a sip from her vodka and tonic.

Mike had threaded a cherry onto the swizzle stick and stuck a sliver of lime on the salt-coated rim of the glass before handing her the drink. Mike was a nice man. He was naturally nice. Conversation washed over her. Surrounding her, but not including her. Nobody seemed to know what to say to her.

It was always the same. She never belonged, no matter where she was. And then it was like her beloved mama was sitting beside her, her downy lip bristling with indignation at this downright humiliation as she muttered, 'Never mind, darling, it's because you are so special. But if you think this motley group is worth your time, go on and make the effort.'

She had never shirked the effort. Jacob, her husband, had

been the result of one such effort to belong. But Jacob was dead and her days stretched once more, empty and hollow, unless she made an effort.

She clinked the ice in her almost empty glass. Had she drunk most of it already and on an empty stomach? It felt good, though. She clinked the ice once more, gleaning curious glances, and then announced to no one in particular, 'I was mugged two weeks ago.'

And then, again, 'I was mugged, you know.'

The swirling conversation whirled to a halt. Eyes stared. Heads turned. A mugging victim who had survived to tell the tale. They moved in closer for the kill.

The sudden attention went to Sarah's head. She gulped the rest of the drink and put the glass down. She cleared her throat, laid her hands on her lap and narrated her story with the composure and eloquence of one who had already aired her adventure several times before.

'It was around four in the evening. I was coming back from the Odd Lot on 50th Street. I was walking towards the Shelter Station on 8th Avenue, humming to myself, when I felt something tug at my handbag. Instead of letting go, I tightened my hold and pulled back. The next thing I knew, I had fallen into the gutter on my face.'

Sarah paused. She knew all about the importance of pausing while recounting a story. God knows what they didn't teach you in schools then, but they certainly honed your elocution skills. Someone, was it Mike, she didn't notice, exchanged her drink for a fresh one. Taking a sip from it, she continued, 'I lay there telling myself, this can't be happening to me. After a long moment, somebody helped me up. It was a security guard from a nearby warehouse. In fact, he'd gone after the mugger and tried to nab him.'

'Is that all?' someone remarked disappointedly. Where was

the blood, the knife wound, the sinister mugger, the excitement of NYPD Blue?

'No, that isn't all.' Sarah's voice rose.

'The police arrived and then the ambulance. A detective took me to the hospital. I could barely stand. I felt so battered and bruised.'

'Dazed, you mean. After all, he hadn't done anything to you.' Kathy, the news reporter in her rushing to the fore, insisted.

'Dazed, battered, bruised, words don't mean a thing, young woman, when you've been mugged.' Sarah spoke coldly.

'Now, now, Sarah, as always, you are exaggerating. And Kathy's right. The mugger hadn't even stuck a thumb in your back,' Yvonne broke in.

'What do you mean, exaggerating? I have bruises all over me. It's still impossible for me to wear a bra the usual way. I have to hook it from the front and then turn it.'

'Oh now, really,' Trudie muttered, boredom already creeping in. Gowri turned to speak to Stephen, and Nisha put her arm through Costa's and led him away.

From the corner of her eye, Sarah saw her audience dwindle, until only Mike was left. She moved closer, suddenly feeling bereft.

Mike sensed the snub that his guests had just subjected Sarah to, and his heart went out to her.

Yvonne, talking to Divakaran, peered over the rim of her glass and watched Mike put his arm around Sarah. She bit her lip. Mike never saw her as vulnerable. She was the strong older woman. Once she had worn miniskirts and her hair to her waist. He'd found her sexy, but never defenceless.

Yvonne squared her shoulders and walked towards Sarah, when Mike moved away to replenish someone's drink. In her coldest voice, she said, 'That wasn't a very nice story. Hardly the kind of stuff that is right for dinner-table conversation. I just hope no one has lost their appetite.'

Sarah started to protest. First, she'd been told she was exaggerating. And now, her etiquette was disgraceful. Then she stopped. What was the use?

She felt despair well up in her. Why had she manipulated herself into this house? She wasn't welcome. Nobody wanted her here. Not even Mike. He'd invited her out of some sense of misguided pity. Her jaws ached with the pain of not being able to cry aloud. Of not being able to say, 'Forgive me, I was just so lonely.'

She had done a despicable thing and was paying for it.

The turkey was carved. Mike felt the steel enter his muscle and rip his tendons.

Plates were loaded, sauces sprinkled, carefully arranged platters disarrayed. Thanks had been said and blessings sought. Now feed the flesh and damn the weighing scales.

Mike stared at the torn remains of the turkey and wondered if he was a cannibal to savour the juices of a creature he had felt so much fellowship with. How could he eat his turkey brother without any remorse?

Chet picked his teeth between mouthfuls.

Subdued and silent, Sarah pecked at her plate. Nobody took any notice of her. It was as if she were a shadow, flitting around with no substance.

The coffee was poured, the cake eaten, and then it was time to go. From the kitchen door she watched Trudie and Gowri do the washing-up. She would have liked to do that. Stand with her elbows in warm water speckled with blobs of fat and scour the plates until they sparkled. And then dry them and lay them on the rack. She would have liked to belong to the Sink

Sisterhood. But no, Yvonne had refused. Too many hands, too many accidents. Anyway, Mike's called for a cab.

And so she waited at the fringes of the evening. When the cab came, Mike saw her into it, kissing her grey, papery cheek defiantly, sadly.

As the cab turned into Broadway, Sarah put her face into her hands and wept. The cabbie pretended not to hear. Many men and women rode his cab every day. Some of them talked to themselves, some read a book, some wept. He didn't have the energy to get involved.

Sarah wept all the way to 70th Street and up the elevator. As she rubbed nourishing cream into her face, tears still ran. Rivulets of rejection from a frozen lake called alone.

The leftovers were wrapped in aluminum foil. Dishes covered with plastic wrap. Ashtrays emptied. Glasses washed. Plates dried. All was quiet and in order.

The couple climbed the stairs of the house they had paid for together. Power-surges had been controlled, energy-levels regulated, sleep-cycles adjusted, and now their lives had fallen into a pattern of meticulous synchronization.

As they lay in bed touching shoulders, their thoughts meandered to the evening. For Yvonne, it was a party ruined. For Mike, it was a vision of bleakness life held for him twenty years from now, in this land where there was no place for the old and lonely.

'Honey,' he whispered, 'next year, let's not invite anybody for Thanksgiving.'

'Why?' she asked.

When he didn't answer, she allowed her anger to surface. 'I didn't say anything to her. Okay, I did snub her a couple of times, but the woman was asking for it.'

'That's it, you see,' Mike said gently. 'You didn't say anything. You treated her as if she wasn't there. You ignored her. You shouldn't have done that.'

'You didn't expect me to welcome her after what she did. Or, did you? And those stockings falling off. Why can't she wear pantyhose like everyone else does? But you can't let her ruin Thanksgiving for us. I thought it meant something to you…'

He felt her turn to her side. She was right. She always was. But within him, the agony he'd seen in Sarah's eyes throbbed. She had contorted her features into a mask from which her eyes had glistened. Black pools in a chalky waste. Would she ever be able to forgive them?

He knew Yvonne would never forgive her. Yvonne hadn't liked seeing what life could be when one was seventy-eight, alone and dependent on social security. Yvonne detested displays of weakness, and Sarah had made an open admission of loneliness. Yvonne liked her blinkers. She liked to see only what she wanted to. And Sarah had tried to take the blinkers off.

Mike stared at the ceiling. Stray images wandered into his mind. Of dreams dreamt eons ago. Of children and a home with picket fences… Memories of a mother who took in strays and taught him to reach out… Of a time when he had been plain Madhavan, and not Mike.

The rhythmic snores jerked him back to reality. In this life, there was no longer any place for such obsolete virtues. He closed his eyes and shut his bleeding heart out. Remembrance was a form of sinning in this world he had chosen to live in.

Sarah went back to her living room and lit the candles. Sabbath was just born. The evening stretched many miles away. She had nothing else to do. So she was going to say her memorial prayers and ask for blessings.

Twenty-four names of people who had left this world, and eighty-nine names of people who knew her and she thought cared for her. Taking time with each name, she tried to remember everything that person had stood for.

And then Sarah did one more despicable thing. She gave up.

She went into the bathroom and shut the door. She filled the bath with water, sliced her wrists with an old razor blade and stuck her gnarled hands into the swirling water, outwitting the ultimate mugger of them all.

Sarah escaped him and his black-petalled tentacles. And the candles continued to burn into the dawn of the day after Thanksgiving.

mercury woman

*A*s time goes by—*Indian woman, 34, well-educated, successful, professional, 5", slim, fit, spontaneous, vivacious, gourmet cook, extra-terrestrial believer looking to share friendship with 36-45 emotionally and intellectually successful loving woman. Laughing, fine dining — belief in alien presence and activity most important. Note/ Photo/ Phone NYM L9OZY*

He flipped the page hurriedly. He didn't want her catching him reading the dating column. He put the magazine back on the stack that had been carefully arranged to show off her multitude of interests. *Art &Antiques*, *Omni*, *Vogue*, *Food and Wine* and on top of it all, the two-month old *New York* magazine. He looked around him with interest. The carefully chosen wallpaper, the profusion of green, the goldfish bowl in which two monster goldfish frolicked, the plump cushions, and the carpet into which his feet sank ankle-deep.

He slipped his shoes off and flexed his sock-clad toes. It had been a long drive and he would probably have to check into a motel for the night on the way back. Unless, of course, her hospitality extended to offering him a bed for the night.

'Would you like a drink?' she asked.

'Yes. Can I help?' He jumped to his feet.

'Thank you. I'll fix it. What will you have? I can offer you

Bacardi, wine or cognac,' she said firmly, moving to stand between him and the mini-bar.

Didn't she trust him to pour a drink for himself without spilling it? Or did she have something in there she didn't want him to see? His father did things like that. Setting aside the Scotch for his close friends, while acquaintances and some associates were given a not-so-expensive whisky. He would have liked a Scotch on the rocks. Ambrosia on the tongue, music in his ears with every clink of ice. 'I'll have the wine,' he said.

'Red or white?' Again the twang. She sounded totally American. What an asset her accent would be when he was entertaining foreign associates.

'Whatever,' he said, eager to please.

The wine tasted sour. He gulped down a mouthful and looked for the nuts he liked to munch while drinking. There weren't any. Instead, there were canapés. He eyed them suspiciously and then ignored them.

'So, what's your job like?' He tossed the question in the air as he fumbled to open a pack of cigarettes.

'You can't smoke in here.' A silky rust and orange caftan came into his line of vision. 'And please don't use the word "job". It sounds like assembling a piece of machinery in a poorly-lit, airless shack somewhere in Taiwan. I have a career and I find it very fulfilling. I am a stylist. Do you know what that is?'

He wanted to slap her hard across her face. Smack that supercilious expression off her face. Bitch. Who did she think she was? He shoved the pack of cigarettes back into his pocket and snapped, 'I do.'

'You do.' She sounded surprised. 'The fashion business is still so underdeveloped in India that I didn't think you'd know much about it.'

He gave her a venomous look. 'I don't know why you think all Indians are hicks. Sure, you have been here for the past fourteen years, but you can't have forgotten everything about India. Actually, the average Indian is better read than your average American,' he said angrily.

'I didn't mean to offend you.' She looked contrite. And just for a moment he felt something fierce shoot through him that obliterated the animosity that had crept into the room. He wanted to draw her into his lap and caress away the hurt in her eyes. She was so tiny, and her hair framed her face in little wisps, making her seem like a little girl.

'How long are you going to be in the US?' she asked.

He could see that she was trying to be pleasant. Why did she dislike him so? He was not a fool. Right from the moment he stepped into her home, he knew she didn't want him there. It was not as if he had barged in uninvited. It had been a decision both their families had taken. The horoscopes matched, the age difference wasn't too wide. If you like each other, we can go ahead and fix it, his parents had said. Meet up with her when you visit the States next and let us know, her uncle had added. When he called her, she asked him to come to her apartment in Manhattan. 'I'd rather we ate in than go out. I'll cook you dinner,' she had offered.

He had been delighted by the promise of her words. But when he called next to confirm the date, she didn't sound too enthusiastic. And this evening, ever since he arrived, she'd either been cold and withdrawn, or difficult and argumentative.

When he was a little boy, there had been a grand-aunt who had bewildered him with her erratic behaviour. One day she was fairy godmother, the next day, a wicked witch. And yet another day, a stone-faced sphinx. 'Don't let her upset you, Gautam,' his mother had consoled him. 'You can't blame her. She's a spinster, and spinsters are very frustrated human beings. When she turns crabby, just ignore her. When she knows she's losing your attention, she'll go back to being the sweet old thing she normally is.'

She was thirty-four. A spinster. I guess I'll have to be patient with her, he decided. He smiled at her, hoping to erase the earlier unpleasantness. 'I'll be here for another two weeks,' he said quietly.

'I hope you like Italian food,' she said.

'I like any kind of food. I'm not a fussy eater at all,' he gushed. His parents had set their heart on this alliance.

As she stood up, the fabric pulled tight across her breasts. He wished she was wearing something a little more revealing. Beneath the caftan, she could have a body like a Horlicks bottle. There was much to be said in favour of the usual 'seeing the girl' business back home. The girl in a silk saree that revealed the curve of her waist, outlined the fecundity of her hips and suggested the fullness of her breasts. See the merchandise before you make up your mind...

On the long drive here, he had woven a little fantasy of what the evening would be like. Tall candles, the fragrance of roses, and she in a little black dress. It would be love at first sight for both of them. And in his mind he had listed a series of topics that would scintillate her intellect and bond them forever.

Instead, here he was doing his best to please. And it still wasn't good enough.

'Did you know that a teaspoonful of neutron star material weighs as much as the whole universe?' she said as she poured olive oil from a voluptuously curvy bottle into a pan.

'I see you are interested in astronomy, Malini,' he said, enjoying the sound of her name on his tongue. He rather liked it; the way it made his tongue dip into the well of his mouth and then rise to knock on his teeth, once, twice. Ma-li-ni.

He peered through the telescope fixed on the tiny balcony that overlooked the Hudson River.

'Oh, you found my telescope. Actually, I use it to say hello to my father.'

He straightened, too startled to speak. Her back was turned to him. Was she pretending to be weird? He decided to play along. 'What does your father do in the sky?'

She laughed, a gay, tinkly sort of laugh. 'I know what you are thinking. That I'm either a raving lunatic or pretending to be one.'

He flushed. 'Of course not,' he said. 'I was just curious, Ma-li-ni.' Dip, knock, knock.

She stopped shredding the lettuce and said pensively, 'I was sitting by his side. He was dying. He'd been dying for a long time. That night, he seemed more frail than ever. And strong at the same time. As if he'd made peace with himself. He held my hand and said, "Darling, you mustn't ever think your daddy's abandoned you. I'll always be there, where you can see me, watching out for you."

'I didn't want him to see me cry. So I went to stand by the open window. And as I stood there, I saw a bluish purple light rise vertically. It hung there in the black sky for several minutes.

'I heard my father whisper my name, but I was so amazed by what was happening in front of me that I ignored him. As I watched, the ball of light shot horizontally across the sky and vanished into the horizon.

'When I turned around, my father was dead. Have you heard of inter-dimension technology? That's what happened. My father passed from one dimension to the other.'

'Are you saying you saw your father become a star?' He almost laughed aloud in disbelief. She really was a weirdo.

'No, I said he exchanged one dimension for the other. What do you think people mean when they say a soul has left for its heavenly abode? Anyway, I don't care what you think. I know I can see my father when I want to. He's always there on the periphery of the horizon, twinkling away at me,' she retorted.

'Next you'll be telling me you believe in UFOs and little

green men from Mars,' he sneered.

She tossed the salad furiously and snapped, 'Nearly three million Americans have reported some kind of extra-terrestrial experience. All of them can't be making it up.'

He saw the rise and fall of tomato cubes, cucumber slices, onion rings, pitted olives and walnut slivers glistening with oil. He wondered if his face was as waxy as the mozzarella. He could smell the garlic and oregano. And basil. What a joke! He imagined the expression that would appear on his mother's face when he said, 'Your future daughter-in-law worships the holy tulsi too. Only, she keeps it in a ceramic jar and uses it to bring out the flavour of the holy cow slaughtered and chopped to a fine mince.'

This was not going to work out. He wished he had the courage to walk out of the room and the apartment. But then he thought of his mother's voice that had quavered as it crossed continents and oceans to pour into his ears. 'Son, she's been alone for so long that she's bound to resent the idea of sharing her life with anyone. Be calm. Be patient. You know how much this marriage is going to help the family business. And you'll be getting a beautiful, intelligent and rich wife.'

When she had paused, he had thought at first that it was the time difference that was making her sound so careful with her choice of words. But as he heard her next sentence, he knew she had been framing it in her mind. 'But that doesn't mean you have to settle for soiled goods,' she said.

'Mother,' he exclaimed. 'I can't ask her if she is a virgin.'

'Of course not.' His mother sounded horrified. Theirs was a conservative family and any reference to sex was strictly avoided. 'I didn't say that. All I meant was, just keep your eyes open and check for any signs of male presence in her life.'

I wish I had fallen in love with the girl next door, he thought a little forlornly. I could have avoided all such complications. But he was here and he knew how much he would regret it for the rest of his life if he didn't seize this opportunity. Ma-li-ni. And so he agreed meekly to what he knew was a preposterous idea. The existence of star fathers and flying saucers. 'I suppose three million Americans can't be wrong.'

He zipped up his trousers, washed his hands and wiped them dry on a pale pink towel. He admired the bathroom fittings and then, in the manner of a professional detective zoning in on his target, he threw open the bathroom cabinet with a flourish.

Spare toothbrushes. Tylenol. A first-aid kit. Tampons. Hair-removing cream. Face packs. And a razor. He lifted the razor to his nose. It smelt faintly of soap. The same soap that nestled in the soap dish. Had she shaved her legs early in the day? Or had her boyfriend left it behind?

He picked up the strips of medicine and examined them. Was she on the pill? There was no evidence to suggest that she was. But she could be using a diaphragm, he thought unhappily.

'Are you looking for something in there?' Her voice crept in through the bathroom door.

He stepped out and found her waiting outside. 'Are you a virgin?' he asked.

Anger flared in her eyes. 'You are incredible, you know.' She looked at him as if she couldn't believe what she was seeing.

He felt the mulish look descend on his face. 'Are you a virgin?' he persisted. 'In India, I wouldn't have to ask a girl this. But...' He shrugged, an American shrug he had picked up in the past few weeks. A gesture he quite enjoyed using. Not only did it contain a wealth of meaning, but it also made him feel very American, very much in control. 'Your situation is different.'

She looked at him thoughtfully. 'Maybe,' she said quietly and then walked away, leaving him to figure it out.

What kind of an answer was that? Maybe. How could anyone be a maybe-virgin?

Tall candles flickered. The room was heavy with the fragrance of spice, lilies of the valley and melting wax. She had laid the table with creamy linen, pottery plates and burnished silverware. There was a bottle of wine and sparkling glasses. Fom the living room, the faint strains of a violin wafted in. It really didn't matter whether she was a virgin or not, as long as she kept house like this every day, he decided.

When the key turned in the lock, he felt a big portion of his intestines descend into his knees. Was there a boyfriend after all? Just as he was feeling generous and forgiving...

Black boots. Black jeans. Black leather jacket. And was that a motorcycle helmet in its hands? He looked at the tall creature in amazement. As he watched, he saw it take off its jacket and shake its long blonde hair. He sighed in relief. It was a woman. He smiled. But she ignored him and went towards Malini. The two women kissed.

Something about the picture they created made him feel like an intruder. As if he had stepped in on a very private moment. They looked so right together. The tall blonde and the petite brunette. Hand in hand. Cheek to cheek.

'Meet my girlfriend and apartment-mate, Ingrid Clark.' Malini introduced her to him in a voice that suddenly seemed full of content and restfulness.

She knew the effect she was causing, but she went on as though she were relishing his embarrassment. 'Gautam doesn't believe in extra-terrestrial activity. See if you can convince him,' she said, caressing Ingrid's cheek.

'I didn't say I don't believe in it,' he began and gave up when Ingrid dropped a book and several pamphlets into his lap. *The Silent Invasion. Paranormal Occurrences. Close Encounters: The True Story...* He pretended to browse through them while he tried to listen in on the stealthily whispered conversation taking place in the kitchen. When he sneaked a look, they had their arms about each other.

They ate quietly, making little attempt at conversation. When they finished, he refused coffee, saying he had a long drive ahead, and it would be best if he left right away.

There was no mention of future meetings. Nor did she offer him a bed for the night. On the highway, he realized with malicious glee that he'd forgotten to ask if he could help with the washing-up. He knew it was expected of him. That was the American way. But it's not my way, he told himself aloud. And as he sped into the night, he phrased the email he would write to her family, telling them exactly what he knew about her.

'If she were a planet,' he began, 'she would be Mercury. Small, virulent and extremely eccentric. There is something about her that would attract any man at first glance. Until you realize that it is impossible for a man to live with her. In her airless realm, there is no room for a man. He would suffocate and die.'

It was extremely scathing and nasty. And totally satisfying as a way of wreaking revenge for the humiliation she had put him through.

Two days before he flew back to India, he received a FedEx package. Puzzled, he tore it open impatiently and found a box of chocolates and a handwritten note on perfumed stationery.

Thank you for telling my family about me. I would never have had the courage to do it myself. Thank you for getting them off my back.

He crumpled the note and tossed it aside. For a moment, he felt like doing the same to the box of chocolates. But they looked expensive. And he hadn't bought his mother anything, yet. She would, he knew, appreciate it.

two out of three ain't bad

Someone—maybe Arun—had drawn a pink heart on a yellow post-it and stuck it on her dashboard. Ila smiled at the pink heart and crumpled it into a ball. If only, she thought ruefully. She had his love and loyalty; as for his body, it was on offer for the pretty young boys he picked up every night.

Ila stood at the entrance of Koshys and pushed the door open. For a moment, the darkness of its interiors licked at her feet. A mire of secret fears bubbled. What if he doesn't turn up? Will I be left waiting at the table? What if I encounter pity in a pair of eyes?

Ila's hands were full. Car keys. Black leather purse. Sunglasses. Mobile phone. By such things as we are known these days. By such things we draw the circumference of who we want to be. Ila was no different. Besides, when her hands were full, Ila didn't have to worry about what to do with them. Rest them at her side? Fold them into a gesture? Let them flutter, loose and awkward? These were accoutrements for Ila to hide behind. To defend her from betraying her nervousness.

She looked at the clock on the farther wall. She was ten minutes early. If she got there before him, she would have time to compose her face into a mask of disinterested charm, she had thought.

She looked around, her eyes sweeping the room. A crowd

of lawyers with the shut-in demeanour of Emperor Penguins on an ice floe; men with a stolen hour, sipping at a stealthy beer; a lone blue-eyed shaggy-haired tourist sprawled on a chair, nursing an omelette and reading a book; a bunch of ferocious-faced women in khadi kurtas and terracotta earrings; a writer holding court; a young couple brushing shoulders, entwining fingers; an old man in a tweed coat, stirring sugar into his cup of coffee…

Waiters, like silver fish scurrying through the pages of an old book, darted between tables. Bottles glinted from the bar at the farther end. Paintings aspiring to be works of art stood frozen on walls the colour of watered-down chicken curry. Fans mounted high above the paintings in gilt frames whirred their heads towards her. Laughter, the clink of cutlery, the scraping of a chair leg and stray words rose up to greet her.

As always, the brown rexine sofa of the corner table by the window beckoned invitingly. She claimed the table for herself, scattering her belongings on it. She slid into place, perched her elbows on the table and stared at the traffic through the window. St. Marks Road trembled and trilled with the early evening traffic.

A waiter hovered. When she looked up, he gushed. Water from a stainless-steel jug. Teatime treats—egg sandwiches, mutton cutlets, cheese cake, apple pie. Friendliness. Are you ready to order, ma'am?

She avoided his eyes. She held the glass of water between her palms and gazed into it as if it were a crystal ball that would reveal her future. She said, 'I'm waiting for someone.'

Ila was thirty-seven years old. An age when most women have got around to acquiring husbands and babies. An age when all women begin to encounter their mothers in their bathroom mirrors. An age when women let the relief of not having to tout for companionship any more fill their insides and show as soft fleshy folds around their middles.

Ila had been waiting for someone to arrive in her life since she was fourteen and had first felt strange longings stir in her. Through college, through her career as an architect, through life as girl to woman, she had been waiting for that someone. With bated breath, with stringent calorie control, with regular workouts, with mind expansion programs and age defying creams, she had been waiting all this while.

When she graduated, her parents had begun scouring the matrimonial pages for a husband for her. Someone who will be just right for you, they said, as they drew circles around suitable prospects with a red-tipped felt pen.

Ila had grimaced.

'I can't do this,' she had said. 'I can't marry a man because his complexion and gotram match mine or his bank balance is healthy and his family pedigree impeccable.'

Her parents sighed. 'Well, it isn't as if we stopped you from finding someone you like. Are you telling us the truth? Is there someone? Something you are keeping from us? We don't mind who you marry as long as you are happy.'

Ila had wanted to burst into tears then. How could she tell them of this strange restlessness that ate her...that clawed, fanged monster that made her turn her nose up at anyone her parents thought suitable?

How could they know what she wanted in a man or of life? They who lived in a quiet leafy cul-de-sac in Cooke Town, in a house they had lived in for thirty-five years. Her parents didn't understand change. Nothing had changed in their lives, or so they believed. This was the street they had always lived on. They didn't see the old bungalows reduced to rubble and the giant trees lying on their side. They didn't see that apartment blocks stood where once lone houses had, and that the roads meandering though this sleepy little section of the city were throbbing with life, restaurants and ATM points. So their daughter was still their little girl who needed to be advised on what to wear, whom to marry and how to live her life, and a koel's call from the crest of the mango tree in the garden was a reminder that all was well with their world.

Ila wondered if she had a congenital failing. Everybody else she knew seemed to fall in love so effortlessly. She really wished she could fall in love. Several times she had thought that she had found him. That incredible man she could grow old with. That someone who would offer her his body, his soul, his time, his hunger… Several times she had discovered that toads remain toads, no matter how often and in how many different ways you kissed them.

She wasn't cynical. In fact, Ila's one fault was that she still believed she was destined to meet that perfect man. And so she wouldn't settle for anything less.

Which is why, after she had put the phone down, she drove across the city from Koramangala to her house and spent most of her lunch hour skimming through the contents of her wardrobe.

Her mother had watched her in amazement. 'Where are you going?' she had asked.

'Is it someone we know?' her father had chipped in.

Ila shook her head. 'No, no, I have a business appointment and what I am wearing isn't right for that,' she mumbled through her teeth.

What is wrong with you, a voice within asked. You are thirty-seven years old and you still have to account for each decision you make?

Ila waited for them to leave her room. She clicked the door shut and began trying on clothes. Permutations and combinations.

Chic, yet friendly. Cool, but nice. Elegant and fun... Ila so wanted it to be right this time.

She took tremulous sips of water. When Ila first began seriously looking for that someone, there was a song she dredged from her teens. It echoed the most furtive of her longings; compulsions she knew she could never voice and yet, the song played within her, an anthem that accompanied her search. *On a hot summer night, would you offer your throat to the wolf with the red rose?*

'My name is Niranjan,' he had said. 'I read the piece you wrote on design in the streets, in the *Design Guide* magazine. I am a designer myself. From NID. In fact, Feroze gave me your number.'

'Yes,' she had murmured. His voice had caressed her secret desires. It was a voice that spoke of copious testosterone and a ribcage like the insides of a cathedral. A voice that bore the inflections of age and the tenor of experience. Ila let herself be seduced by the possibilities the voice held, now that credibility and professional compatibility had been established. The song played in her head: *Would he offer me his mouth?*

'I was wondering if we could meet,' the voice tantalized. 'I don't live in Bangalore,' it added with an urgency that drummed within her as well.

'Oh!' she murmured. *Would he offer me his teeth?*

Then, petrified that he would think it sounded like a rebuff, she said hastily, 'Sure, I would love to.'

'Where?' The question hung between them. 'You tell me,' he said. 'You are the native. I am just visiting...'

'Let me think. Hmm...' *Would he offer me his jaws?*

'I could come over to your place,' he suggested.

'I have a better idea. How about Koshys? Do you know Koshys?' she asked, not wanting to meet him alone the first time. *Would he offer me his hunger?*

'Oh yes. What time?'

'Half past four?' *Again, would he offer me his hunger?*

'How will I know you?' she questioned.

'I think I'll know you when I see you. But if it's going to be of any help, I carry a khaki bag with leather strips on its sides,' the voice smiled.

'I'll look forward to seeing you then,' she whispered, feeling shooting stars travel up her spine. *And would he starve without me?*

Ila was anxious these days. Her biological clock was ticking away at a furious pace. Each month she reached for a packet of sanitary napkins, wondering if it was the beginning of the end. The last man she had gone out with was a client. A wolf in a St. Bernard's clothing. They had sat beneath a gigantic moon, crunching pappadums that came with the cocktails. She sipped at her daiquiri and told him of her reiki sessions while he stared morosely into his whisky tumbler.

'I was just thinking how long it's been since I had such a nice time with a woman,' he began abruptly. 'At first, my wife and I were so close. Not any more. We live in such different worlds. She does her thing, I do mine. There is nothing more between us these days,' he said, reaching out to capture her hand in his.

Ila wanted to scream. Not again. Not bloody again. Until she had experienced it, she hadn't believed that married men resorted to clichés, particularly worn-out ones such as this, expecting it to produce results. Or was it her? Did they think she was so lonely that any man, married or otherwise, could bed her?

She got through the evening, extricating herself with minimum damage to her person and dignity. At home, she made herself a cup of malted milk and settled down to watching *The Ghost* on Star Movies. When the tears began to fill her eyes, she told herself she was crying because of the movie and not because she was afraid that this would be the pattern for the rest of her life.

The right kind of man was so difficult to find. She went to parties, picnics, theatre festivals, and once even a Hasher's Run... Men of her age, no matter how much they enjoyed her companionship, wanted only one thing—girls with slender haunches, dewy complexions, and wide 'will you show me the world' eyes. As for the younger men, they wanted passion without strings, and maybe a pizza thrown in free. Not that Ila had men standing in a line clamouring for her attention—Hey Ila, look at me! No Ila, I got here first!

Ila looked at her watch. It was twenty minutes to five. Once Koshys had had two doors, one at either end of the restaurant. Now there was just one.

The door opened. She sat up straight. She sucked her gut in and pushed out her chest. She looked at her trouser suit and wondered if she should have worn something more feminine. A salwar kurta? Except that she always felt such a frump in one.

She didn't look thirty-seven. She didn't look twenty-two either. She licked her lips, tasting lipstick and trepidation. *Will he offer me his mouth?*

He must be twenty-four, she thought as he stepped in. Khaki bag, flannel shirt, faded jeans, designer stubble, searching eyes... So young that she would want to cut his lamb cutlet for him into neat sections and fork them into his mouth. So naive that if she were to flick a crumb off his upper lip with her short but immaculately groomed nail, he would flush in embarrassment and then gloat within that she had made a pass at him. So goddamn gauche that in a few moments of sitting across the table and taking his second sip of liberally sugared coffee, he would ask in that devastatingly attractive older-and-experienced-man voice of his, 'I heard you handle retail merchandising in your firm. I was wondering if there is a vacancy for a designer like me in your firm?'

He began to weave his way through the tables towards her. For a brief instant, she was tempted to linger. Just for a brief instant. Then she gathered her belongings hurriedly and stepped across the room, into the shadow of a pillar, and slipped out before he had even spotted her.

In the car, she took Arun's pink heart, smoothened the creases and wedged it back on the dashboard. Her mind shifted gears and moved to another song from the same album—*Two out of three ain't bad*. On her way home, she stopped at the florist and asked for a spray of orchids to be delivered to her home. It was always nice to open the door and discover a bouquet of flowers, even if you had paid for it yourself.

behe-moth

how easy it is to dismiss me as a creature of no consequence. Yes, my dear friend, even you do it. The truth is, most people think they know everything there is to know about moths. It's all been recorded, transcribed and even published.

There isn't much to know about someone like me—stout body, dull colouring, seeking to let the hues of the wood resin me to the shadows, aching for the comfort of woollens and dusty musty books. Enough printer's ink has been spent on describing me and what is the usual mortal course of existence: birth, metamorphosis, youth, search for a mate, babies, and eventually death, either by time or an accident...which is why I think it is time I told you my story. As I know it.

First, there is the little matter of history. It isn't as if one morning I woke up from uneasy dreams to discover that I had become a giant insect. On the contrary, a laboratory created, unwittingly I admit, a biological jigsaw of me. In this world populated with genetic jumbles and me-toos, I do not know if it was the tail of a Y chromosome or the leg of an X chromosome that turned me into what I am. A creature that resembles a moth but is anything but moth-like. I do not even know if I have an X or a Y, or any chromosome.

Moths will travel halfway across the world, lured by the siren song of the female moth's pheromone. My ancestor was no different. Except that he grew tired of being enticed by artificial pellets that promised much and delivered nothing; rather like firing blank shots into an inflatable doll, if you see the point. And so he chose to set out in search of an insignificant but real pheromone. A kind of King Arthur seeking the Holy Grail, vessel, receptacle. Unknown to him, he carried a trace chemical that tried to fuse with his inside code and finally found its homing place in me. All this is speculation, but there is nothing I can do beyond hypothesize why I am what I am.

So I was born, and like Bheeshma in the Mahabharata, I've been around. Modern science, even if it created monsters like Dolly, Lure, mothballs and deodorants has its uses, chief among them the television. Which is why, for a moth, my sense of the mythical is real.

Moths don't live long. I have; I continue to. I wonder why. As life goes past me, it seems that while everything has changed, I alone continue to remain impervious to age and time.

Sometimes I watch my brethren seek and hover around a light and I see them reduced to lifeless bodies singed by the flame. How brief is the brush with glory. And I think: no matter what, I shall never be devoured by that need to cast a gigantic shadow.

I live in a room. Once it was a house that old man Costa lived in. Costa's skin glowed a translucent white, beneath which the veins stood out. Blue-green veins; blue-green as the sea his ancestors had chosen as their pathway to this alien and pagan land. They came in fine ships and chose the finest virgins to have their babies. Then they left, leaving behind little half-Portuguese babies with milk-white skins and Roman Catholic souls. Costa searched for a bride whose skin would match the translucence of his own, with veins blue-green as his, in which red blood would course. Fecund, and with hips that flared plump as a cashew apple's, she would bear his babies and they would keep alive the bleached remnants of their combined ancestry.

When he found her, Costa married Marie and took her away to his home. He had a huge house and enough money and wanted nothing from Marie's family. Besides, he didn't like the brown cast that shadowed the skin of some of her family. Every now and then Costa would hold his palm alongside Marie's and compare their skins. That their complexion was identical increased his lust for her, and soon a baby arrived.

Costa was at his export firm when Marie felt the pain gather in her hips. The midwife was sent for and when she arrived, Marie was led to the room prepared for the birth. Costa rushed home. His palm was sweating with the heat, he told himself, rather than fear. He tapped a cigar against a wooden balustrade and put it into his mouth. He groped for a match and then forgot all about it when he heard Marie's scream. The veranda outside the birthing room was long and shadowed. The afternoon heat pressed down upon the red tiles, but Costa continued to stand there. He chewed the end of the cigar and spat the tobacco out. His hands were shaking so badly that he couldn't light a match if he tried.

Then he heard the wail, a lusty long one, and Costa smiled. The midwife opened the door and stuck her head out. 'You have a daughter,' she said. 'A healthy girl. And the mother is fine too. You can come in a little while.'

Costa decided he would call his daughter Alberta; his great-grandfather, who had sown the seed of whiteness in their blood, had been called Albert. But when Costa saw the baby's brown skin, he paled. 'I've been cheated,' he thought. How could the baby have a brown skin; even her lips had a brownish cast. The children that would be born to her would be black as cashew grease, he thought. That night he left his house by the sea and moved inland to Bangalore, where the British had chosen to build a cantonment. The sun here was pale and watery and didn't scorch the skin. The houses had granite walls, parquet floors and chimney breasts. The Anglo-Indian women had brown hair and skin as pale as his and Costa found it as natural to lose himself in their arms as he found it to light a fire on cold evenings. But when the women whispered, each one of them, 'Hey man, when are we getting married? Mummy was asking if I am a kept woman or what,' Costa felt a crinkling of his insides. He missed Marie then. Besides, he was a Catholic and divorce was out.

So, when the baby was a year old, he sent for his wife. 'Don't bring the child,' he said. Marie came to him and in his house surrounded by trees—mangoes and avocados, figs and guava trees; jasmine and rose bushes; geraniums and asters; vines and creepers—he made love to her again and again. He sent her away to have the baby and said, 'It hurts me to tell you this, but if its skin is like yours and mine, bring the baby with you. Otherwise, come back in a year's time, alone.'

Seven times Marie went back and forth. Alone. Then Marie died and the children grew up, reared by benevolent aunts on tales of a father who was much too busy to see them. In the lushness of the garden, I watched and waited to see if Costa would seek his children out. But he was a stubborn man and he grew old without ever seeing his children.

The house was old and decrepit, but I loved it. The living room with its musty sofas, a carpet patterned with mildew and an upright English piano was my home. No one sat on the sofas or played the piano. I liked its fragrance of age and neglect. In that room, I had a sense of the past. There was a painting there. Of a girl sitting on a bench. Strange flowers framed her face and you could almost hear the rustle of leaves above her head. The sky was blue and cloudless and her lips were parted as if she were just about to lick their dryness away with her tongue.

I liked to perch on the painting. Every day, I would choose a new spot. One day I fed at the girl's lips, another day I rested on her thigh. And yet another day, I lodged myself in the curve of her palm. She was mine to do with as I pleased and in this pleasant manner, I spent many a month.

Once every day, Costa would totter into the room and touch his possessions with a sad caress. He would stop by the painting, leaning heavily on his stick, and stare at it. I could see a wistfulness in his gaze. Who was she, I wondered. Did he know her? Or was she a dream, like she was for me? I would flutter away and hide behind the curtain when Costa came into the room. Not that it mattered. He would just wave his hand and do nothing more. But I felt as if I was intruding. It was his home and I respected that. I was, after all, a trespasser.

Unlike butterflies, the fashion models of the Lepitoptera order, I don't flit around. I stay put. And so I was there when the blood stopped coursing in Costa's blue-green veins and he fell to the ground, clutching his chest and pawing the air with broken sounds. The children arrived and wandered through the rooms. They had no memories of this house; besides, the Mother Superior of a rather well-endowed order of nuns had offered to buy it. The Mother Superior was an aunt twice removed and it seemed less treacherous to sell the house to a convent. Each one of the children took a keepsake from the house and I watched my beloved painting being crated away. Soon the house was razed and a women's hostel came up in its place.

I chose to make my home where the living room used to be. And there I have remained, watching time toil ceaselessly, carrying on its twin legs the changing course of curtains and people's faces.

It isn't easy being me and it wasn't easy then. Unlike other moths who knew what it was to hear the song of the pheromone and seek satiation in a mate, I had yet to encounter the aria that would make me want to abandon everything and drown myself in it. So I amused myself by watching the inmates who lived in the room.

Then there came a young woman. My mouth filled with scale-like dust. She was the girl in the painting. Or so it seemed. But there was none of that serenity of expression the girl in the painting had. This one seemed agitated and unhappy.

The room was furnished, but she curled her lip at what was there, and set about creating a womb for herself. She hung heavy drapes on the windows and lit low lamps. A new mattress was laid over the old one. She went out to work and spent the rest of the time wrapped in a quilt. On her face was the tightness of expression I had seen on moths who'd tired of life. A glassiness that stole into their eyes as they wished their breath away. Who or what was she mourning?

I watched her day and night. I watched her day and night and thought of old man Costa and I knew for the first time what it must have been like for him. Of how his desire for Marie couldn't surmount his horror of the brown babies... It wasn't right, just as it wasn't for me to love a woman. She didn't have the right pheromone and so I was content to look at her and think of her as the girl in Costa's painting.

One night she opened a suitcase and drew out a flagon of perfume. The flagon was in the shape of a woman. Or perhaps a man with shoulders rounded with guilt and remorse. Its cap was jewel green and it glowed as though a firefly lived in it. She opened the cap and sniffed it. Her face twisted. Then slowly, as though she were in a dream, she dabbed it on her pulse points; behind her ears and between her breasts, at the crook of her elbow and the curve of her knee. And then she lay back in bed, flung the quilt to the floor and began to weep.

I breathed in the fragrance. My feathery antennae quivered. A slow warming. The stringing of desire. The plucking of senses. A quartet played an aria I had never heard before and then I could bear the tympanic beat in my head no more. From behind the curtain I emerged and let the pheromone beckon.

How does a moth seduce a woman? It is against the laws of

nature. But if you remember, the laws of nature don't hold good for me. So I flew in through the thick layers of darkness and perched on the headboard, waiting for her to fall asleep. I held my wings extended by my sides, ready to swoop down. I felt myself grow...

Do you know what a moth's wings feel like? Like exquisite jacquard against your cheek. Like a peacock feather trailing down your spine. Like the fur of a peach on the inside of your lip. Like moss on a wall brushing the soft underside of your knee. Like a tendril of hair curling into your ear. Like these and a million things more that unleash a cataclysm of feelings, I hovered and teased, fed and numbed my senses and hers. Then I went back to the curtain and as all moths do, I rested. I folded my wings and wrapped them around my body.

I was overwhelmed by what I had done. I was afraid. What had I let loose within me?

Next day, the woman moved out. She said that ever since she had come here she felt as if someone was watching her. All day and all night. That eyes followed her every move and sometimes even crept into her thoughts. 'After last night, I think I am going to lose my mind. I dreamt that a phantom loved me. The truth is, it was the most beautiful lovemaking I've known, but it was eerie. You know what I mean,' she told someone on the phone. 'Can you imagine how desperate I must be, to dream that a phantom teased my body with moth-like caresses... So I've decided that I need to get out of here. Actually, I need to find a new life. If you want, you can have this place.'

She left some things behind, including the flagon of perfume. The new woman was different. She put up light voile drapes and preferred the old hard mattress. Her mouth seemed even harder. The floors crawled with cushions and an occasional magazine. I didn't like her very much until the night there was a storm and the power went off. She didn't know what to do.

So she lit the candle the earlier one had left behind and then drew out the flagon of perfume from its place.

The aria sang again.

Soon the room acquired a reputation for being haunted by a spectre. Not a presence that flung objects or threw open closed windows or trod heavily. The room was haunted by a spirit of restlessness, the women who lived there said. No one stayed for more than a month or two. The hostel warden placed a mirror on the door and hung wind chimes near the window. No one thought of throwing the perfume away. Good perfume was hard to find and every new occupant succumbed to it sooner or later.

And in the morning, she would awaken to a sense of unease. Some discontent too. I had travelled in the night on the wings of the aria and so had she, and as my calling card I had left pale silvery dust that clung to the paths we had travelled together. The dust, remnants of my nocturnal trails, crept into her bloodstream and made her want more than she had. It made her wish she were somewhere else. That was both my blessing and my curse.

The room has remained unoccupied for a while now. When I miss my women, I think of what Sartre said: Hell is the other. I would quote that aloud and chuckle to myself.

Mostly, I like being alone. In the silence, I have begun to think of the room as my own. In its emptiness, I practice pirouettes and swallow flights. Free-falling and flitting.

Each day I pretend to be someone. One day I am the Count of Monte Christo and another day I am Casanova. If I am Don Juan one Monday, the following Monday I'm Krishna. The day it rains, I am Indra and on 4 July, I'm Rhett Butler. These are games I play to amuse myself.

I have learnt to forget and remember. To resist and succumb. To wait with my wings folded till the aria sings again.

the madness of heracles

for many days now, I have been coming to this place. It is on the Street of Darkness. A street lined with chambers where we may do things which we are not allowed to do otherwise. On the left is the House of Courting. A nest of cubicles where young couples are permitted to hold hands and kiss. Diagonally opposite is the Chat Room where one may sit and chat via the internet or with a mobile. In our city, citizens are not allowed private internet access and all mobiles are sold minus the texting service.

Then there is the Wear What You Want Stop where I am told young girls go to wear clothes they are not permitted to wear on the streets or to their colleges. The Smoking Corner is a fug of cigarette and cigar smoke, the stink of beedi and the aroma of pipe tobacco. The Artist's Box is where artists may paint what their souls really yearn to, with the additional solace of hanging their creations up for a while, knowing they will not be dismissed as unsaleable or vulgar or too personal…

So many chambers, each one of them allowing us, for a brief while, to be who we really want to be…

We are a moral people and we must not flaunt our appetites, society tells us. Which is why, every evening we watch, on each one of our 809 TV channels, sagas that advocate moral behaviour. The eyes of our women fill with tears as they watch heroines cast aside all self-respect and become slaves to everyone else's needs. Our men puff with pride, thinking their place in society is secure as long as women will let these tears roll down their cheeks. And our politicians grow quietly large, knowing that as long as we are a people who do not know what we want, we will remain powerless. Meanwhile, our young sneak away to the Street of Darkness...

The chamber of secrets, as the neon lights call it, is where the young come to dream. Of who they could be if they were not call-centre executives or software engineers or BPO employees. I am an aberration here, but it is only here that it is possible for me to set aside the present and think... I think of all that has brought me here. It wasn't so long ago.

They tell me I went mad. That I spoke my mind instead of restraining it within a cloak of decorum as a man of my stature ought to have. They tell me that I spread terror through the land. That there was no knowing if I was hero or villain because I did everything I shouldn't have. They tell me that·for a while, it was impossible to open the newspapers or go on-line without seeing me on the party circuit with a drink in my hand and a fag in the other. That I displayed a total disregard for the bureaucracy and politicians. They tell me that I pulled apart the secret life of my rival with my pen and left it exposed for people to draw conjectures from. That I broke all laws of humanity which decreed every man ought to be allowed to be a hypocrite. They tell me I questioned all the norms and dictates. That I demanded to know why we were turning into what we had been a thousand years ago, and denounced the new moral code that we had evolved for ourselves. They tell me it was my excesses that led to this. Or perhaps it was my excesses that brought about the curse: to be a creature who didn't know what he was doing.

I remember now the contempt I saw on their faces. The

disgust and revulsion my presence evoked in them. All who had once sought me out turned their heads away. I had dared question our lives, their lives... I braved it out. I, who had feared nothing in my life, wasn't going to permit society to turn me into a pathetic kowtowing worm. But I had forgotten what isolation can do to a man... Even heroes need the occasional assurance of a friendly smile, the affectionate clasp of a hand, the inflection of companionship in a voice... I may have been the archetype of the indomitable man, but I fell short of divinity in wanting human warmth. If I had been older, would I have survived it? I do not know. I never will, because I walked away from the dark chamber I had shut myself in.

I so wanted to belong again.

From a writer I became a television producer. They even found me a title. That was to be my punishment. For twelve years I was to perform whatever labours were set before me. Family dramas. Lifestyle features. Interiors and chat shows. Cookery and made-up reality shows... It is too painful for me to recount every detail of that period. All I can say is that these labours drove out every single bone of pride in me, and covered me with glory and self-disgust. Everywhere, they talked of the feats I had accomplished. The eyes that had turned away from me now dogged my every step like faithful hounds. I was a hero again in their eyes. In mine, I was nothing.

The years have been spent and I have returned. This is my home now, my heaven, they tell me. Even my father wants me at his side. And I am my mother's favorite son now.

I stand at the Olympian gates of the condominium I live in, the porter of this heaven, and watch the gods and goddesses return. I banquet at the divine tables, theirs and those of the city nobles. I am one among them; every shred of my being pulsates with the resonance of a complicity that lets me belong. Only somewhere deep in my heart, I know again that mortal phantom stalking amidst this twittering society, with his pen drawn.

I may never write again, but I shall not stop seeing.